MW01170706

Eyes of Destiny

The Journey of Almanza

Ms. LJ Hall, PhD

Morgan Pacific Publishing

Copyright © 2024 by Ms. LJ Hall, PhD

Published by Morgan Pacific Publishing Conyers, GA, Imprint of Morgan Pacific Publishing

Identifiers: Library of Congress Control Number: 2024925055 Paperback ISBN 979-8-9920740-0-0

All rights reserved. No portion of this book may be reproduced in any form without written permission from the publisher or author, except as permitted by U.S. copyright law.

This is a work of fiction. Names, characters, places, and incidents are either the product of the author's imagination or used fictitiously. Any resemblance to actual persons, living or dead, or actual events is purely coincidental. This publication is designed to provide accurate and authoritative information in regard to the subject matter covered. . While the publisher and author have used their best efforts in preparing this book, they make no representations or warranties with respect to the accuracy or completeness of the contents of this book and specifically disclaim any implied warranties of merchantability or fitness for a particular purpose. Neither the publisher nor the author shall be liable for any loss of profit or any other commercial damages, including but not limited to special, incidental, consequential, personal, or other damages.

For permissions, contact: Morgan Pacific Publishing   by email: publishing@morganpacificpublishing.com

Author Bookings: booking@msljhall.com

This book was created with assistive tools used to edit, refine, and error-check the content, as well as to generate illustrations that enhance the visual storytelling.

Eyes of Destiny
Journey of Almanza

Morgan Pacific
Publishing Company

Dedication

To Sumner, Jai'Ana, Olivia, A'Raya, Lola, Ja'Leyah, Harley, and Lily—you hold my heart; I love you endlessly. (Listed in order of age not love)

To the incredible women in my life who shaped me: thank you for your strength, wisdom, and light. A special thanks to Susie Morgan and Constance Candie, who poured so much love into me as a child—I hope I am making your heavenly spirits proud.

And to every young girl, teenager, and woman who feels abandoned or alone: you are unique, and you are powerful beyond measure. You are a light in this world, and you can become anything you desire. You are worthy, and the world is waiting for you to rise. Keep fighting.

Prologue

In a land touched by ancient magic and hidden mysteries, where towering baobab trees held secrets whispered by the winds, there lay a village called Shongwe. The people of Shongwe were bound by tradition, their lives shaped by age-old tales and silent reverence for unseen forces. Yet, even in a place of such stillness, destiny stirred beneath the surface, waiting to change the course of their world.

It began with Nandi, a young woman of quiet strength and fierce love. She defied the rules of her tribe, binding herself to a prince of a rival clan. Their love, powerful and forbidden, was shadowed by tragedy when the prince fell in battle before ever seeing the daughter he would leave behind. This daughter, born with piercing green eyes and a presence that unsettled the elders, would carry the weight of her lineage and more.

Named Almanza, meaning "beautiful," the child was both a blessing and a mystery. Her emerald eyes, striking and otherworldly, seemed to hold within them the wisdom of centuries. To the people of Shongwe, however, they were seen as a sign of misfortune. The village elders whispered of a curse, fearing that Almanza's arrival would bring ruin upon them all.

Driven by love and desperation, Nandi was forced to make an agonizing choice: abandon her child to protect her, or face banishment and danger. Clinging to hope, she carried Almanza far away, journeying under starlit skies until she reached the village of Maputo. There, beneath the branches of a mighty baobab tree, she entrusted her child to fate, leaving her with a prayer for safety, a promise of love, and the strength of a mother's heart.

Yet, fate had plans beyond Nandi's wildest fears and deepest hopes. Almanza would be found by Queen Adisa, Maputo's wise and compassionate ruler, who, in that tiny infant, saw a daughter the ancestors had chosen for her.

Raised in Maputo, Almanza would grow into a child of light and power, her gifts a wonder and a secret both. But even under the queen's protection, her unusual gifts would spark whispers and stir fears that would shape her path.

And so, the journey begins—a tale of sacrifice, courage, and the unfolding of a destiny bound to a love that defied the boundaries of tribes and fear itself. For Almanza was not just a child; she was a guiding star in the world's ancient sky, carrying within her the promise of both danger and destiny intertwined.

CHAPTER ONE

The Birth and the Curse

LONG AGO, IN A land where the sun graced the earth with golden warmth and the stars painted the sky with boundless wonder, there was a village called Shongwe. Nestled deep within a lush valley, Shongwe was a place of life and harmony. Ancient baobab trees towered over its borders, their twisted branches sheltering the homes of the villagers like guardians of old. The people of Shongwe lived with a rhythm as steady as the seasons, guided by traditions that had endured for centuries.

For Nandi, life in Shongwe had been a tapestry woven with vibrant threads of joy and the occasional dark strand of pain. She loved the mornings when the village stirred to life. The soft bleating of goats, the crackling of fires, and the laughter of children as they raced through the open fields filled her with a sense of belonging. She cherished the evenings most of all, when the sun melted into the horizon, and the entire village gathered under the stars to share stories, sing songs, and dance in honor of their ancestors.

Yet, Nandi had always felt a restlessness, a yearning for something beyond the confines of Shongwe. This longing had led her to Kahlil, the prince of a rival tribe. Their love was as passionate as it was forbidden, born of whispered promises and stolen moments under the moonlight. When Kahlil was taken from her, her world had dimmed, but from that pain came a spark of hope—her child, Almanza.

On the night of Almanza's birth, the moon was full, its light spilling over the village like a silver blessing. Nandi labored alone in her hut, her cries muffled by the thick walls of woven reeds. The village midwife had come and gone, her work done. Now, Nandi held her newborn daughter in trembling arms, overwhelmed by the silence that followed the child's arrival.

She looked down at Almanza's tiny face, searching for signs of life. Just as fear began to tighten its grip, the baby opened her eyes.

At first, they were a warm honey-brown flecked with gold, like pools of sunlight. But as Nandi gazed into them, they began to shift. The brown deepened, the gold brightened, and within moments, her daughter's eyes became a green so vibrant it seemed to glow. Nandi felt a shiver run through her—a mixture of awe and unease.

"Almanza," she whispered, her voice trembling. "You are my light."

The next morning, Zola arrived with a basket of herbs and a steaming pot of porridge. Her steps were brisk, but when she saw the baby in Nandi's arms, she paused.

"Nandi," she said, her voice careful. "She... she's beautiful."

"Why do you hesitate?" Nandi asked, her tone sharper than she intended.

Zola set the basket down and moved closer, her gaze fixed on Almanza. "Her eyes... they're unlike anything I've ever seen. The village will talk."

"They already do," Nandi replied bitterly. She had heard the murmurs as she fetched water earlier that morning. Women huddled together, their whispers following her like shadows. "Let them talk. She is my daughter, Zola. No one can take that from me."

Zola placed a hand on Nandi's shoulder, her grip firm. "You're strong, Nandi. But you know how the elders are. They see anything they don't understand as a threat."

"They don't understand love, then," Nandi said, her voice breaking.

As the days passed, the atmosphere in Shongwe grew colder. Nandi remembered the joy she once felt walking through the village square, where traders sold baskets of fruit and spices, and children wove flower garlands to place on the ancestors' shrine. Now, those same villagers avoided her gaze. Mothers pulled their children close when she passed, and even old friends turned away, their expressions clouded with fear.

But not Zola. One afternoon, she found Nandi sitting beneath the great baobab tree, where they had spent countless hours as children. Zola joined her silently, handing her a woven blanket.

"They're afraid," Zola said after a long silence.

"Of a child?" Nandi asked, her voice heavy with disbelief.

"Not of her," Zola said softly. "Of what they think she represents."

Nandi looked at her friend, tears brimming in her eyes. "When did we become a people so afraid of the unknown? Our ancestors taught us to find strength in each other, to honor the mysteries of life. Now they cower like children in the dark."

Zola sighed. "Fear can turn even the wisest hearts cold. But Nandi, you're not alone in this. You have me."

It wasn't long before the whispers reached the ears of the elders. Summoned to the central clearing, Nandi stood before the council as the entire village gathered to watch. The air was thick with tension, the kind that precedes a storm.

Elder Sefu, his voice a blend of authority and weariness, spoke first. "Nandi, daughter of Shongwe, your child's eyes are not of this world. Such signs have always brought misfortune to our people. We must act to protect the village."

"She is just a child!" Nandi protested, her voice ringing out.

Elder Masego stepped forward, her expression stern. "She is more than that. Her presence is a disturbance, a disruption to the balance we hold sacred."

"She is my daughter," Nandi said fiercely, her arms tightening around Almanza. "And she is no curse."

The crowd murmured, their faces a mixture of fear and pity. Only Zola stood firm, her gaze unwavering as she stepped forward.

"She is no threat," Zola said, her voice steady. "And Nandi has done nothing but love her child. Are we so quick to cast out our own?"

The elders ignored her, their focus on Nandi. Elder Sefu's voice was grave. "You must choose, Nandi. Surrender the child to us, or leave Shongwe forever."

That night, Nandi sat beneath the great baobab tree, her thoughts tangled with memories. She remembered the way the village celebrated her coming of age, the way they mourned with her when her parents passed. This was her home, her heart. Yet, as she looked down at Almanza, sleeping peacefully in her arms, she knew her path was clear.

When Zola approached, her eyes glistened with unshed tears. "You're leaving, aren't you?"

Nandi nodded. "I have to. She deserves a chance to live free from fear."

Zola knelt beside her, pressing a small leather pouch into her hand. "For the journey. Herbs for strength and protection. And remember, no matter where you go, you are not alone. I will find you."

Nandi pulled her friend into a fierce embrace, her tears soaking into Zola's shoulder. "Thank you," she whispered.

Under the cover of darkness, Nandi left Shongwe, her heart heavy but resolute. She carried Almanza close, her steps guided by the moonlight filtering through the trees. The village she left behind grew smaller with each step, but her resolve grew stronger.

"Almanza," she whispered to the sleeping child. "We will find a place where love is not a curse. Where you can shine as brightly as you were meant to."

As she disappeared into the night, the baobabs stood silent, their ancient roots holding the secrets of the land—and the promise of a mother's unbreakable love.

Guided by a love that overwhelmed her soul, Nandi chose her daughter's safety above her own. "Am I wrong for this?" she murmured, her voice barely above a whisper. "Creator, is this truly the path you've chosen for me? For my child?" She closed her eyes, a single tear escaping down her cheek. "If I am mistaken, if my love has led me to the wrong choice... then forgive me. But I have no other way to protect her." She gathered Almanza in her arms and, under the cover of darkness, ventured away from Shongwe, away from all that she knew.

Through the night, she journeyed, her bare feet treading across soft grass and through a mystical forest that seemed alive with whispers. The trees, tall and ancient, swayed as if sharing in her sorrow. The moon's light filtered through their leaves, casting a silver glow on the path before her. As she walked, a deep regret settled within her, like roots twisting into her heart, and she whispered lullabies of love and protection to the tiny life in her arms.

A Mother's Love

ARRIVING AT THE EDGE of Maputo under a soft, pink-tinged dawn, Nandi held her sleeping daughter close for what would be the last time. The air was cool, and the gentle rustle of leaves filled the silence. Before her stood the ancient baobab tree, its twisted branches stretched wide, reaching out as if to welcome Almanza. The ancient baobab tree rose before her now, its sprawling branches silhouetted against the fading sun. Its roots spread wide, weaving through the earth like the fingers of a guardian. The air here was different—cooler, softer, carrying the faint scent of blooming wildflowers. Maputo, the village she had heard of in hushed tales, lay just beyond the tree. Nandi had heard the tales of the baobab's power, its spirit a guardian of those who had no one else to protect them. She whispered a prayer to the tree, hoping it would take Almanza into its care and watch over her child with the strength of the ancestors.

The villagers had spoken of Maputo as a place of refuge. It was said that the lost, the forsaken, and the abandoned could find safety there. Nandi prayed it was true.

She reached the base of the baobab and collapsed to her knees, her body trembling with exhaustion. She carefully unwrapped Almanza from her chest, laying her on a blanket she had woven during quieter times. The baby stirred but did not wake.

"My sweet girl," Nandi whispered, brushing a curl from Almanza's forehead. Tears fell freely now, dotting the fabric of the blanket. "This is where our paths part. I am leaving you here not because I want to, but because I must."

11

Almanza's tiny hand flexed, and Nandi gently held it, savoring the warmth for what she knew would be the last time.

"You are destined for greatness," she said, her voice breaking. "One day, they will see you for the gift you are."

She reached into the folds of her garment and retrieved a smooth, round stone. The memory of the woman who had given it to her rose unbidden.

It had been midday in the desert when Nandi stumbled, her legs finally giving out. The sun beat down mercilessly, and her vision blurred with heat and tears. She collapsed to the ground, clutching Almanza as if the child alone could anchor her to the earth.

A shadow fell over her, and she squinted up to see an elderly woman wrapped in vibrant red and yellow cloth. The woman's eyes were sharp, her presence commanding despite her frail frame.

"Child," the woman said, her voice steady, "why do you wander the desert with a baby?"

12

Nandi struggled to sit up. "I'm taking her to safety," she said, her voice hoarse.

The woman studied her for a long moment, then nodded. "The desert is harsh, but it also reveals strength. You are braver than you know." She reached into a pouch at her waist and pulled out a small stone.

"Hold this when your burden feels too great," she said, pressing it into Nandi's palm. "Let it remind you of your purpose."

Now, Nandi placed the stone beside Almanza. "This is part of me," she said softly. "Carry it with you, my little star."

A rustling sound made her freeze. She turned sharply, her arms instinctively reaching for Almanza.

"Peace," a man's deep voice said. "We mean no harm."

Two figures emerged from the trees. The man was tall, his shoulders broad and his face lined with years of work under the sun. Beside him was a woman with kind eyes and a brightly colored shawl.

"Who are you?" Nandi asked, her voice trembling.

"I am Jabu," the man replied. "And this is my wife, Mara. We live here in Maputo."

Mara's gaze fell on Almanza, her expression softening. "The child..." she whispered. "She glows."

Nandi stiffened. "She is my daughter," she said firmly. "I've brought her here to give her a chance at life."

Jabu nodded. "You've come far," he said gently. "Your journey tells a story of great love." Mara knelt beside Almanza, her hands hovering above the baby as though afraid to disturb her. "What is her name?" "Almanza," Nandi replied softly.Mara smiled. "A beautiful name for a beautiful child. She carries something special." "They called her a curse," Nandi said bitterly. "My village wanted to hide away her." Mara's expression turned fierce. "She is no curse," she said firmly. "She carries the light of the ancestors." Jabu placed a hand on Nandi's shoulder, his grip warm and steady. "You've brought her to the right place," he said. "Maputo is a refuge for those who need it."

Nandi's knees buckled, and she sank to the ground. "I'm so afraid," she admitted, her voice breaking. "Afraid I've failed her. Afraid I've abandoned her."

Mara wrapped an arm around Nandi, her touch gentle. "You've done the hardest thing a mother could do," she said softly. "You've given her a future."

Nandi looked at Almanza, now cradled in Mara's arms. The baby cooed softly, her green eyes glowing faintly in the dim light.

"She will grow strong here," Mara continued. "The baobab will watch over her, and the village will love her. One day, she will make you proud."

The red bird perched above suddenly took flight, its vibrant wings cutting through the twilight. Nandi watched it go, feeling as though it carried a piece of her soul with it.

"You are brave, Nandi," Jabu said. "A mother's love is the strongest force in the world."

Mara nodded. "And one day, Almanza will know the depth of your sacrifice."

Nandi smiled, feeling the warmth of Mara's words settle deep within her heart. The red bird, perched proudly above, continued to sing, its vibrant feathers glowing brightly in the morning light. Nandi felt a tear slip down her cheek—not of sorrow, but of joy, as the weight of her decision seemed to lighten. Perhaps this was what she had been waiting for—a sign that she had chosen the right path for Almanza.

With newfound strength in her heart, Nandi nodded slowly. " Thank you," she whispered, her voice barely audible. " Thank you both. You don't know how much this means."

Mara beamed at her, squeezing her arm in an affectionate gesture. " Of course, child. We are all connected—by blood, by spirit, and by fate. The child will find her place in this world, just as the stars find their places in the sky."

Nandi continued her journey. Suddenly, a gust of wind rustled through the trees, stronger than before, and Nandi felt it rush around her, lifting her hair like a gentle caress. It was almost as if the wind were carrying her love forward, pushing her hopes and dreams toward the sleeping child. She closed her eyes and let herself feel, for one last time, the pull of motherhood—the instinct to protect, to hold, to shield. But then she felt the weight of responsibility and the ancient fears that surrounded Almanza's birth, settling like stones in her heart, reminding her of why she had to leave. Nandi pressed a trembling kiss to Almanza's forehead.

As Nandi turned to leave, the red bird took flight, its wings a blur of color against the golden morning sky. She watched it go, feeling as though it carried a piece of her heart with it.

She walked away slowly, her steps heavy but resolute. Each one took her further from the life she had dreamed of with her daughter, but closer to the hope that Almanza would be safe, loved, and destined for greatness.

Under the shade of the baobab tree, Almanza stirred in her new guardian's arms, a soft coo escaping her lips. The woman smiled down at her, her heart already full of love for this little star who had been left in their care.

Nandi did not look back again. The journey ahead was long, but the knowledge that Almanza was in good hands gave her the strength to keep walking, even as her heart ached with every step.

"Goodbye, my little star," she whispered. "Shine bright, even when I cannot see you."

"Creator, protect her. Let her find kindness in this village, let her heart be filled with love, and let her spirit grow strong."

As the forest faded into the distance, Nandi whispered to the wind, as if sending a final prayer for her daughter's future.

"Goodbye, my little star. Shine bright. And if there's a way, I will always find you. I will always love you."

As she walked away, the desert stretched before her. But for the first time, her steps felt lighter.

" Ancestors, have mercy," she whispered, her voice trembling as she paused to catch her breath. " If there is any forgiveness for a mother's heart, grant me peace. I did what I thought was right, what the seer said was necessary... but will I ever find solace?"

CHAPTER THREE

The Journey Back Home

NANDI'S FEET DRAGGED AS she approached the village. The past weeks had been a blur of endless travel, sleepless nights, and relentless self-doubt. Now, a faint sense of hope stirred in her chest as she saw smoke curling upward from clay chimneys and heard the faint sound of children's laughter. She tightened her shawl around her shoulders, willing herself to keep moving.

At the edge of the settlement, she paused, suddenly unsure. Her heart thudded as a group of villagers noticed her and began to whisper among themselves. A tall woman stepped forward, her hands on her hips, her expression one of cautious curiosity.

"Greetings, traveler," the woman said, her tone guarded but not unkind. "You've come far, it seems."

"Yes," Nandi replied, her voice hoarse. She cleared her throat and tried again. "I've been traveling for weeks. I'm searching for rest, just for a little while. If it's not too much trouble."

The woman's gaze softened, and she exchanged a glance with a man standing nearby. "We don't turn away those in need," she said. "I'm Abena. Come, let us find you some water and food."

Relief washed over Nandi as Abena led her into the village. The settlement was modest but thriving, with neat rows of huts made from clay and thatch, and a central square where villagers bustled about their tasks. Children darted past, giggling as they chased one another, their laughter carrying on the wind.

As they reached the square, a boy ran up to Abena, tugging on her skirt. "Mama, who is this?"

"This is a guest, Kweku," Abena said, resting a hand on his shoulder. "She has traveled a long way. Can you help fetch some water for her?"

Kweku nodded eagerly and dashed off toward a nearby well.

Abena guided Nandi to a shaded area beneath a large tree. "Sit here and rest. You look like you've been through quite the ordeal."

"I have," Nandi admitted, lowering herself onto the ground. Her legs trembled with exhaustion, but the cool shade was a balm.

Moments later, Kweku returned with a clay jug of water, which he handed to Nandi with a shy smile. She took it gratefully, drinking deeply as Abena watched her with a mix of curiosity and sympathy.

The days that followed were a blur of kindness and tentative hope. The villagers of Lebombo—the name of the settlement—welcomed Nandi with open arms, giving her a small hut to rest in and simple tasks to help her integrate into their community.

Abena became a steady presence in her life, guiding her through the rhythms of village life. They worked side by side in the fields, grinding grain, and weaving baskets, sharing stories and laughter.

One afternoon, as they rested under the shade of a tree, Abena turned to Nandi with a curious look. "You've told me little about yourself," she said. "Where are you from, and what brought you here?"

Nandi hesitated, her fingers toying with the hem of her skirt. "It's... a long story," she said finally. "I come from a village far from here, called Shongwe. And before I came here, I was in Maputo."

Abena raised an eyebrow. "Maputo? That's a place of great renown. The queen is said to be wise and kind."

"She is," Nandi said, her voice soft. She stared at the ground, unsure how much to reveal.

Abena studied her quietly. "You left something behind, didn't you? Or someone."

Nandi's breath hitched. "I did," she admitted, her voice barely above a whisper. "I left my daughter. It was... the hardest thing I've ever done."

Abena's expression softened, and she reached out to touch Nandi's hand. "I can't imagine the pain you've carried. But sometimes, the choices we make out of love are the ones that hurt the most."

Tears welled in Nandi's eyes, but she blinked them away. "I only hope she's safe and happy. That's all I want."

As the weeks turned into months, Nandi began to find a sense of belonging in Lebombo. She formed bonds with other villagers, sharing meals, stories, and laughter.

Kweku became especially attached to her, often following her around with endless questions.

"Nandi," he asked one day, "do you think it's true that the queen of Maputo has a daughter with green eyes who can heal people?"

Nandi froze, her heart skipping a beat. "What have you heard about her?" she asked carefully.

"They say she's a princess now," Kweku said. "Mama says she's a child of destiny."

A lump formed in Nandi's throat, but she forced a smile. "It sounds like she's very special," she said, her voice trembling slightly.

That night, as she lay on her mat, she thought about Almanza and the life she was building in Maputo. The knowledge that her daughter was safe and loved filled her with a bittersweet ache.

Over time, Nandi grew stronger, both physically and emotionally. She threw herself into the work of the village, finding solace in the steady rhythms of daily life.

One evening, as she and Abena sat by the fire, Nandi found herself smiling for the first time in what felt like years.

"You've come a long way," Abena said, noticing her expression.

Nandi nodded. "I have. And I owe so much to this village—to you. I don't think I could have made it through without your kindness."

Abena smiled. "We all need each other. That's how we survive."

Nandi stared into the flames, her thoughts drifting to Shongwe. "I think I'm ready," she said quietly.

"Ready for what?"

"To go home," Nandi replied. "I need to see my village again. To find closure."

Abena's smile turned wistful. "Then go. And know that you'll always have a home here in Lebombo."

The journey back to Shongwe was long, but Nandi felt a newfound strength guiding her steps. The desert no longer seemed as vast or as unforgiving. Each step brought her closer to the place where her story began—and where, perhaps, it would continue.

When she finally arrived at the edge of her village, she paused, taking a deep breath. The sun was setting, casting the familiar landscape in hues of gold and crimson.

"I'm home," she whispered, a tear slipping down her cheek.

She stepped forward, ready to face whatever awaited her, her heart filled with both trepidation and hope.

As Nandi stepped into Shongwe, the memories came rushing back like a flood, overwhelming her senses. The village looked much as it had when she left, with its clay huts clustered together and the fields stretching beyond.

Yet, there were changes too—new huts, unfamiliar faces, and a faint weariness in the air that hadn't been there before.

The sight tugged at her heart, a mix of nostalgia and trepidation. She paused by a cluster of baobab trees that bordered the village, her fingers brushing the rough bark of one as if seeking reassurance.

"Ancestors, give me strength," she whispered, her voice trembling.

A child playing nearby noticed her first. His eyes widened, and he darted off toward the village, shouting, "A stranger has come!"

Nandi felt the weight of curious gazes as villagers emerged from their homes. Some approached cautiously, while others stood back, watching her with a mix of wariness and recognition.

"Nandi?" a woman's voice called, tentative but tinged with familiarity.

Nandi turned to see an older woman stepping forward, her gray-streaked hair tied back in a simple wrap. It was Akua, a neighbor from her youth, now aged but still carrying the same sharp eyes and determined stride.

"Akua," Nandi said softly, her lips trembling into a smile.

The older woman gasped, her hands flying to her mouth. "By the spirits, it is you!" She rushed forward, enveloping Nandi in a tight embrace. "We thought we'd never see you again, child. Where have you been?"

"It's... a long story," Nandi replied, her voice thick with emotion.

Before long, a small crowd had gathered, murmuring among themselves as they observed her. Some faces were kind and familiar; others were new and cautious. Akua, sensing Nandi's discomfort, took charge.

"Come, Nandi," Akua said firmly, gesturing toward her hut. "You need food and rest before we talk of anything else."

Grateful, Nandi allowed herself to be led away. Akua's hut was warm and welcoming, filled with the comforting scent of herbs and the soft hum of everyday life.

As Nandi sat down on a woven mat, Akua placed a bowl of steaming porridge in front of her. "Eat," she urged. "You look like you've been through a storm."

Nandi hesitated for only a moment before taking a bite. The taste brought tears to her eyes—simple, nourishing, and deeply familiar.

As the evening wore on, Akua and Nandi sat by the fire, the flickering flames casting long shadows on the walls.

"Nandi," Akua began gently, "what happened all those years ago? You vanished without a word. The elders spoke of curses and shame, but I always believed there was more to your story."

Nandi took a deep breath, her hands twisting in her lap. "There was," she admitted. "I left because... because of my daughter."

"Your daughter?" Akua's eyes widened.

"Yes. Almanza," Nandi said, her voice trembling with both pride and sorrow. "She was born under circumstances the elders would not understand. They said she was cursed because of her green eyes, and they wanted her gone. I couldn't let that happen. So I took her far away, to a place where she might have a chance at life."

Akua leaned back, her expression thoughtful. "You sacrificed everything for her."

"I did," Nandi said, tears welling in her eyes. "And not a day has passed that I haven't thought of her. I hear she's safe now, being raised as a princess in Maputo."

Akua's eyebrows lifted in surprise. "The green-eyed princess of Maputo? That's your daughter?"

Nandi nodded, a faint smile breaking through her tears. "Yes. The villagers here called her cursed, but in Maputo, she is a blessing."

Akua reached out to squeeze Nandi's hand. "You did the right thing, Nandi. A mother's love is the greatest gift. And now you're back. Perhaps it's time to heal the wounds of the past."

The next morning, word of Nandi's return had spread throughout Shongwe. Some villagers approached her with warmth and curiosity, eager to hear her story, while others kept their distance, their expressions wary.

Nandi spent the day visiting familiar places—the stream where she had played as a child, the fields where she had worked alongside her neighbors, and the hilltop where she had once gazed out at the horizon, dreaming of a brighter future.

As she walked, she encountered old friends who welcomed her with open arms and shared memories of happier times.

"You haven't changed much," teased Kwame, a childhood friend with a grin as wide as the river.

"And you haven't grown up at all," Nandi shot back, laughing for the first time in what felt like years.

Later that afternoon, a gathering was held in the village square. The elders, seated in a semicircle, called Nandi forward to speak.

"Nandi," said Elder Sefu, his voice deep and commanding, "your return is unexpected. We have heard whispers of your journey and the child you bore. Tell us, what brings you back to Shongwe?"

Nandi stood tall, her heart pounding in her chest. "I have come to find peace," she said. "I left because I had to protect my daughter. The circumstances of her birth were misunderstood, but I see now that leaving was not just to save her—it was to save myself. I carried shame and fear, but I am no longer afraid. I am proud of the child I bore, and I am proud of the woman I have become."

The square fell silent, her words hanging heavy in the air.

Finally, Elder Sefu spoke again, his tone softer this time. "You have been through much, Nandi. And though your path has been difficult, it seems the ancestors have guided you back to us. Let us not dwell on the past, but look to the future."

The villagers murmured their agreement, and Nandi felt a weight lift from her shoulders.

Over the following weeks, Nandi settled back into life in Shongwe. The village, once a place of pain and judgment, became a place of healing and renewal.

She formed bonds with new friends, rebuilt old relationships, and found joy in the simple pleasures of daily life. But most of all, she found strength within herself—a strength she had always carried but had only just begun to recognize.

Each evening, as she sat beneath the stars, she whispered a prayer of gratitude to the ancestors and a silent message to Almanza:

"I love you, my daughter. And I will always be with you, no matter how far apart we are."

CHAPTER FOUR

A Queen's Heart

NOT FAR FROM THE baobab tree, Queen Adisa, the beloved ruler of Maputo, was taking her early morning walk through the village outskirts. Her presence was graceful and commanding, her rich, colorful robes adorned with golden symbols that gleamed in the early light. Her thick, coiled hair was wrapped with beads and gold, each piece symbolizing her lineage and connection to the ancestors. Her steps were purposeful, but this morning, an inexplicable urge pulled her toward the baobab, as though an unseen hand guided her path.

As she approached the tree, her eyes fell upon the small bundle resting at its base. A sense of wonder mixed with caution filled her heart as she knelt, her hands reaching out to pull back the soft cloth that wrapped the child. When she saw the baby's face, Queen Adisa gasped. Almanza's eyes fluttered open, revealing the striking green that held a depth and mystery unlike anything she had seen.

" Who are you, little one?" she whispered, almost as if speaking to the heavens. She looked up, sensing the presence of something beyond her, something sacred, watching over this child.

As if in response, the red bird appeared, settling onto a branch just above Queen Adisa's head. It chirped softly, its song filling the air around them, and the queen felt a warmth blossom in her chest, as though this moment had been destined by the ancestors themselves. She looked back down at the child, her heart swelling with an unexplainable protectiveness.

" Is this your doing, Creator?" she murmured, her gaze lifting momentarily to the sky. " Have you sent this child to me? If so, I promise I will raise her with all the love and wisdom I possess." She looked down at Almanza, the little girl's green eyes staring back up at her, as if listening, understanding. " You will be safe here, child. In this land, you shall be loved."

The bird's song grew louder, as if blessing her words, and Queen Adisa felt a peace settle over her. She wrapped Almanza in her arms, lifting her gently from the ground, and held her close. The baby nestled against her, eyes slowly closing as she drifted back to sleep, and Queen Adisa knew, with a certainty that surpassed words, that this child was meant to be hers.

" From this day on, you are Almanza," she said softly, " a princess of Maputo." With one final look at the baobab, Queen Adisa turned, carrying the child toward her home, the red bird's song following them through the dawn.

Queen Adisa sat in her grand chamber, holding Almanza close as the baby slept peacefully in her arms. The soft glow of lanterns illuminated the room, casting warm light over the intricate tapestries that adorned the walls, each one depicting a chapter of Maputo's history. The queen gently stroked Almanza's cheek, marveling at the tiny life cradled against her chest. She could hardly believe that it had only been days since she found this child beneath the ancient baobab tree.

Adisa gazed down at the child, a sense of awe filling her. "You came to me as if by fate, little one," she whispered. "What are you, and what have you brought into my life?"

Her voice softened as she looked into Almanza's serene face. "I have longed for you... and here you are, filling my heart with a joy I never thought I would know again."

Yet, beneath the joy, a shadow of worry lingered. Those striking eyes! Almanza'a eyes seem to change between a rich mix warm honey of brown and green, sometimes with flecks of gold to a striking green bright and vibrant that still offered warmth of bright glow. There was whispers among the villagers. Adisa could feel the beginnings of fear in her people's hearts. She had ruled Maputo with compassion and strength, but she knew too well how quickly fear could grow if left unchecked. She leaned her head back, closing her eyes as a silent prayer formed in her heart.

"Creator, guide me. Give me the wisdom to protect this child and to protect my people from their own fears. She is a gift—I feel it in my soul. Help me to see her light, even if others cannot."

A gentle knock at the door interrupted her thoughts, and Adisa opened her eyes, turning to see her trusted advisor, Omar, enter the room. She waved him in, grateful for his presence.

"Come in, Omar," she said, motioning for him to sit beside her. "You look as though you have something on your mind."

Omar took a seat, folding his hands in his lap. His voice was gentle, but his tone held the gravity of his concern. "My queen, the villagers are curious... and also concerned about the child," he said carefully. "They do not understand who she is or where she came from. Her green eyes alone... they worry that she may bring change they aren't prepared for."

Adisa's hand instinctively tightened around Almanza, and she cast a protective glance at the sleeping child. "They have no reason to fear her, Omar. She is just a baby, innocent and full of life."

Omar nodded, his eyes sympathetic. "I know, my queen. But you know how fear can grow in the unknown. If they come to see Almanza as different, as something beyond their understanding, it could lead to unrest. People may try to reject what they do not comprehend."

Adisa's voice grew firm, a fierceness in her tone that only a mother could possess. "Then they must learn to understand, Omar. This child is my daughter now. I will raise her to be a leader filled with kindness and strength, and I will not allow anyone to bring harm upon her."

Omar smiled, his expression softening. "I have no doubt, my queen, that you will raise her well. But Almanza's path will be filled with challenges that none of us can foresee. You must prepare her for these trials, so she may rise above the fear of others."

Adisa looked down at Almanza, her gaze softening. "I will teach her everything I know. She will be wise and strong, but most importantly, she will be loved." Her voice dropped to a whisper, more to herself than to Omar. "I will not let her feel the loneliness I have known."

As Almanza Grows: Discovering Her Powers

The weeks turned into months, and Adisa dedicated herself to raising Almanza. The child grew quickly, her curiosity boundless, her spirit as lively as a spring breeze.

Adisa nurtured her daughter's kindness, teaching her the values of the court, the traditions of their people, and the wisdom of compassion. Yet, as Almanza's powers began to show, Adisa's awe was shadowed by caution.

One evening, as they strolled through the palace gardens, Almanza, now five, ran ahead, her laughter ringing out like music. Adisa watched her with pride, until suddenly, Almanza stopped, her gaze fixed on something lying on the ground.

"Mama!" she cried, her voice filled with concern. "Look, this bird... it's hurt!"

Adisa joined her, kneeling beside the small bird with crumpled wings lying still in the grass. She placed a comforting hand on Almanza's shoulder. "Sometimes, my love, the creatures of this world fall ill or suffer. It is the way of nature."

Almanza shook her head, her bright green eyes wide and intense. "But I can help it, Mama. I can make it better." Before Adisa could stop her, Almanza reached out, touching the bird gently. As soon as her fingers brushed the feathers, a soft, golden light glowed from her hand, warming the air around them.

Adisa's breath caught as she watched the light grow, enveloping the bird. Her heart raced, torn between amazement and fear. As the glow faded, the bird stirred, its wings unfurling as it regained its strength. With a sudden flap, it took flight, soaring above them with a renewed vigor.

Almanza turned to her mother, her face alight with joy. "Did you see that, Mama? I made it better!"

Adisa knelt down, pulling Almanza into a fierce embrace. "Yes, my darling, you did something truly amazing." Her voice was thick with emotion, and she held Almanza close, feeling the power of her daughter's gift but also the heavy burden it brought.

As she looked into Almanza's shining green eyes, Adisa felt a whisper of fear. This power—this light within Almanza—was beautiful, yet she knew it was something that would set her daughter apart from others. She stroked Almanza's cheek and whispered, almost to herself, "May the Creator give me the strength to protect you, to guide you in the way that is best."

That night, after tucking Almanza into bed, Adisa returned to her chamber, her mind filled with the events of the day. She walked to the window, gazing out at the moonlit village below. Her heart was heavy with the realization that her daughter's gifts, as wondrous as they were, would not be easily accepted by others.

Speaking softly to the night, Adisa whispered, "Creator, you have entrusted me with a precious gift. Help me teach her, help me show her the way. Let her power be a blessing, not a burden."

She paused, drawing in a steadying breath as she looked back at her sleeping daughter. "I will protect her with every breath in my body. But I will also prepare her for the world beyond these walls, a world that may not understand her light."

And as the days turned into years, Queen Adisa kept her vow. She watched Almanza grow, nurturing her gifts and her heart, determined that her daughter would one day walk confidently in her own light, ready to face whatever the world might bring.

The village of Maputo was a place of vibrant life and enduring spirit, nestled in a valley lush with fertile fields and surrounded by verdant forests that stretched to the horizon. From dawn until dusk, the air was filled with the laughter of children, the rhythmic beat of drums, and the distant, melodic hum of villagers singing as they worked. In the mornings, the village awoke with the aroma of freshly baked flatbreads and spiced stews bubbling over open fires, each family contributing their unique recipes passed down through generations. Painted clay pots adorned with intricate patterns lined the walkways, each one a symbol of family pride and artistry.

The people of Maputo took great joy in the simple pleasures of life and held tightly to traditions that connected them to their ancestors. They wore brightly colored fabrics, woven in intricate patterns that represented their family histories and personal strengths—symbols of resilience, wisdom, or creativity. Festivals were frequent, often held in celebration of the changing seasons, births, and marriages, with villagers gathering in the central square to dance and share food beneath the light of countless lanterns strung between the trees. Evenings were marked by storytelling, with elders sharing fables and proverbs under the stars, their voices rising and falling with the crackling of the bonfire.

Though humble, Maputo was known as a place of warmth and generosity. The villagers believed in the power of community and kindness, and no one was ever left to struggle alone. If a family faced hardship, neighbors would bring baskets of food, clothing, or medicines made from herbs gathered from the forest. It was in this atmosphere of unity and joy that Queen Adisa reigned, loved by her people as much for her compassion as for her wisdom.

Queen Adisa's chambers were a testament to her royal heritage and her connection to Maputo's traditions. The grand room was adorned with tapestries depicting the village's history, each thread woven with colors that told stories of past leaders and significant events. Clay lamps, decorated with symbols of the ancestors, filled the room with a warm glow that seemed to embrace Adisa whenever she held Almanza close. Worn cushions and delicate wood carvings of animals and ancestors' spirits lined the shelves, symbols of protection and wisdom handed down through generations.

Sitting in this chamber with Almanza in her arms, Adisa felt a deep and abiding love that she had never known before. It was a love so fierce and consuming that it often took her by surprise, leaving her both joyful and vulnerable. She would gaze down at the child, marveling at her innocent face, the softness of her cheeks, and those mesmerizing green eyes that seemed to hold the mysteries of the universe. The weight of her role as a mother settled heavily on her heart, entwined with the duties of her crown.

There were moments when Adisa's heart would swell with such pride and protectiveness that she felt she could face any threat that might come for Almanza. Yet, beneath her courage lay a tremor of fear that she could never quite shake. She was the queen, a symbol of strength and wisdom, yet the fragility of love made her feel exposed, vulnerable. What if she couldn't protect Almanza from the world's cruelty? What if the whispers and fears of her people grew too strong?

Sometimes, late at night, when the village was quiet and her guards stood watch outside, she would pace the chamber with Almanza sleeping in her arms, speaking softly to the ancestors as if seeking their counsel. "What path awaits her, ancestors?" she would whisper. "And will I be enough to guide her? I fear not the sword, nor the weight of the crown, but the harm that unseen fears may bring to her."

Queen Adisa had always been a woman of confidence and conviction, yet with Almanza, her heart was torn between pride and dread. She saw greatness within the child—a spark of something unexplainable that promised power and wisdom beyond her years. Adisa had no doubt that, one day, Almanza would grow to be a leader who could inspire and protect the people of Maputo. But this gift, this power... it was something the villagers did not understand, and Adisa worried it might one day bring harm to her beloved daughter.

The villagers, as kind and joyous as they were, held deep-rooted beliefs in the spiritual and the supernatural. Although they loved and trusted their queen, Adisa knew that even the gentlest heart could be swayed by fear of the unknown. And Almanza, with her emerald green eyes and mysterious powers that were already beginning to show in small but wondrous ways, was very much an unknown.

Adisa's love for Almanza was unbreakable, yet it brought with it a burden she had never anticipated. To her people, she was a ruler, a beacon of strength, but as a mother, she was vulnerable, open to pain and loss in ways she hadn't imagined. She knew that she must protect Almanza not only from physical harm but from the potential fears and misunderstandings that could arise from the child's differences. She wanted to shield Almanza from every whisper of doubt and every shadow of prejudice.

In those quiet, reflective moments, Adisa would hold Almanza close, her protective instincts mingling with a fierce determination. She would look down at the child and promise, silently but with all her heart, "I will prepare you, my daughter, to face a world that may not understand you. I will give you the strength to walk your own path, but I will also protect you from the storm."

Adisa's love for Almanza became both her greatest joy and her deepest fear. She knew that one day, her daughter would need to confront the power within her and the world around her. Until that day, Adisa would be there as her protector, her guide, and her mother, loving her fiercely and without reservation.

As the days passed, Adisa's resolve grew. She would dedicate herself to guiding Almanza, helping her grow strong, wise, and unbreakable. Maputo was a place of peace and kindness, and Adisa would do everything within her power to ensure that Almanza's light would shine brightly, even if shadows lay in the road ahead.

CHAPTER FIVE

The Power of the Green-Eyed Child

ALMANZA WAS A JOYFUL, curious child who seemed to radiate warmth wherever she went. Her laughter was a familiar sound in the village of Maputo, a place where vibrant flowers bloomed in every corner, large trees spread their branches to create cool, shady spots, and villagers bustled about with kindness in their hearts and smiles on their faces. The air was often filled with the sounds of villagers singing as they worked, children's laughter ringing out as they played, and the rustle of leaves in the breeze, which seemed to follow Almanza wherever she wandered.

Almanza's presence seemed to bring a gentle magic to the village, though most didn't know how to describe it. Flowers bloomed more brilliantly when she touched them, their colors brighter and petals softer. The animals of the village were drawn to her, the stray cats curling up at her feet, the birds perching on her shoulders without fear. Even the trees seemed to respond to her touch, their leaves rustling as if whispering secrets in a language only she could understand. The villagers watched her with a mix of awe and caution, uncertain of what it all meant but captivated by her gentle spirit.

At just five years old, Almanza's world revolved around two close friends, Nia and Kofi. Nia, a bright-eyed girl with a contagious smile and a love for exploring, was Almanza's confidante and her steady friend. With her hair adorned with colorful beads that clicked together as she moved, Nia's cheerful presence was a constant source of joy. Kofi, on the other hand, was a mischievous seven-year-old with a knack for adventure. He was lanky and quick, always challenging the others to race or daring them to climb the tallest tree. His mischievous grin could light up a room, and though he sometimes teased Almanza, he was fiercely loyal.

One sunny afternoon, the three friends were playing near the village's outer edge, where fields of wildflowers swayed in the breeze. The air was alive with the buzzing of bees and the distant chirping of birds. Kofi, feeling particularly adventurous, spotted a small, gnarled tree nearby and picked up a rock, aiming for one of its branches.

"Watch this!" he called to Nia and Almanza, his face alight with the thrill of a new game. With a playful flick of his wrist, he threw the rock, but as soon as it left his hand, he saw a flash of red among the leaves.

"No, Kofi!" Nia gasped, realizing too late what was about to happen.

The rock struck the branch with a dull thud, and with a flutter of wings, a small red bird—a familiar friend to the children—fell from the tree, tumbling to the ground. Kofi's eyes widened in horror as he rushed over, his heart sinking when he saw the little bird's wing hanging at an odd angle.

"Oh no... Red Bird," he whispered, his voice shaky. Though he was usually a strong-willed child, Kofi's face filled with worry. Red Bird was a friend to all the children, a protector who had once swooped down to scare away a snake that had slithered too close to Kofi as he climbed a tree. Kofi loved Red Bird just as much as Nia and Almanza did, and now he had hurt her. He knelt beside her, guilt pooling in his chest as he looked down at the injured bird.

Nia placed a comforting hand on Kofi's shoulder, her own eyes filled with sadness. "It was an accident, Kofi. You didn't mean to."

Kofi nodded, but he couldn't shake the heavy feeling. "I have to tell Almanza," he murmured. He knew she would be heartbroken, but he also knew that she would want to help.

He hurried to find Almanza, who was by the stream, watching the fish dart back and forth with a look of pure delight. When he reached her, he took a deep breath, his voice trembling. "Almanza... I hurt Red Bird," he said softly, guilt thick in his tone. "It was an accident, but... I think her wing is broken."

Almanza's bright green eyes widened with concern, and she quickly rushed to Red Bird's side. Kneeling beside the injured bird, she reached out a hand, her face a mixture of worry and compassion. Her fingers brushed against Red Bird's wing, and for a moment, she simply sat there, her eyes filling with tears.

As the first tear slipped down her cheek, Almanza's eyes began to glow with a soft, mysterious light, their green depths shimmering with an otherworldly radiance. She placed her hand gently over Red Bird's wing, her touch light as a feather. The glow from her eyes intensified, casting a warm light over the bird. The air around them seemed to still, and even Nia and Kofi, usually full of energy and chatter, watched in silent awe.

A single tear from Almanza's cheek fell onto Red Bird's wing, and as it did, a soft, golden light spread across the bird's feathers. It was as if the tear carried a part of her spirit, her love and sorrow intertwining to form a gentle power that wrapped around Red Bird like a warm embrace. The children held their breath, the glow enveloping Red Bird and slowly, miraculously, her wing began to mend.

The bird shifted, her injured wing lifting slightly, then fully extending as if it had never been broken. Red Bird let out a soft chirp, her wings fluttering as she tested her strength. With a joyful cry, she took to the air, circling above the children before landing on Almanza's shoulder, nuzzling against her cheek in gratitude.

Almanza's face broke into a smile, her eyes still shining with the remnants of her glow. She reached up to gently stroke Red Bird, her voice filled with wonder. "I helped her. I really did," she whispered, her heart swelling with both joy and a new, unnameable power.

Nia and Kofi exchanged awestruck glances. They had always known their friend was special, but seeing this—seeing her heal their beloved Red Bird with nothing more than a touch and a tear—left them speechless.

Nia's eyes sparkled with excitement as she stepped closer. "Almanza, that was incredible! You have a gift!"

Kofi nodded, his earlier guilt melting away, replaced by admiration and pride. "You're amazing, Almanza. Red Bird is flying again because of you."

Almanza smiled shyly, looking down at her hands as if they were foreign to her. She had always felt a connection to the world around her—the flowers, the animals, the wind—but this was the first time she realized she could bring healing and life. Her heart fluttered with excitement, yet deep down, she felt a small, uncertain weight. She didn't fully understand this gift, but she knew it was something precious, something she would have to protect.

As the three friends stood by the stream, Red Bird chirping happily on Almanza's shoulder, a breeze rustled through the nearby trees, swirling around them as if celebrating the little miracle they had just witnessed. The village beyond bustled with life, unaware of the magic that had unfolded, but the bond between Almanza, Nia, and Kofi deepened that day, a silent promise to protect one another and the mysterious power Almanza carried.

From that day on, the three friends grew closer than ever. Nia and Kofi vowed to keep Almanza's secret, knowing that her gift was something beautiful, something to be cherished and safeguarded. And as they walked back to the village, side by side, Almanza looked up at the sky, wondering what other mysteries her powers would reveal and what her destiny might hold.

As the children began their walk back to the village, they were filled with an excited energy that made their steps light and their voices bright. Kofi's guilt had melted away, replaced by awe and a growing admiration for his friend. Nia skipped along beside Almanza, her eyes wide with amazement as she kept glancing at Red Bird, who perched happily on Almanza's shoulder, her feathers shimmering faintly in the light.

Kofi scratched his head, grinning in wonder. "Almanza, I thought you were amazing before, but now... now you're like a real healer! How did you even know how to do that?"

Almanza shrugged, looking down at her hands with a soft smile. "I didn't know. It just... happened. I saw Red Bird hurt, and something in me felt like it had to help. It was like my heart knew what to do, even if I didn't."

Nia's face lit up with excitement. "That's what makes it so amazing! It was like magic—no, it was magic! Maybe the spirits of the trees and flowers gave you this power, or maybe the ancestors themselves chose you."

Kofi leaned closer to Almanza, studying her intently. "Did it feel strange when your eyes glowed? I've never seen anyone's eyes do that before. They were so bright... like emeralds in the sun. Even Red Bird was glowing!"

Almanza laughed softly, still adjusting to the awe in her friends' eyes. "I felt... warm. Like the light wasn't just in my eyes but in my whole body. I don't know how to explain it—it just felt right."

Kofi's curiosity only grew as they continued down the path. "Do you think you could heal other things? Like a hurt animal or a broken tree branch? Or even..." he paused, his voice dropping as his mind spun with possibilities, "a person?"

Almanza's brow furrowed as she considered the thought, a trace of uncertainty mingling with her joy. "Maybe. I don't know yet... I don't even understand how I did it this time. I think... I think it only works when my heart feels it—when I really, really want to help."

Just as Almanza finished speaking, Kofi's older brother, Sefu, came down the path toward them, his arms crossed and an eyebrow raised. He had heard snippets of their excited conversation and was watching them with a smirk.

"What's this about magic?" Sefu asked, his tone half-skeptical, half-intrigued. "You three sound like you've discovered a hidden treasure."

Kofi grinned up at his brother, eager to share the wonder they'd just witnessed. "It's true, Sefu! Almanza healed Red Bird's wing with her touch. I threw a rock, by accident," he added quickly, "and it hit Red Bird. Her wing was broken, but Almanza... she touched her, and her eyes glowed, and bam! Red Bird was healed."

Sefu snorted, shaking his head in disbelief. "You really expect me to believe that?"

Just then, Red Bird fluttered her wings, taking off from Almanza's shoulder with a small burst of speed. As she soared over their heads, her feathers gleamed with a soft red glow, leaving a faint, shimmering trail behind her.

Sefu's eyes widened, his jaw dropping as he watched the glowing bird disappear into the trees. He glanced back at Almanza, noticing for the first time the faint sparkle still lingering in her green eyes, a hint of magic that shimmered like stars. He was speechless, and a new respect, tinged with wonder, filled his gaze.

"Okay... maybe I believe it now," he murmured, looking at Almanza as though seeing her for the first time. "But this... this is unbelievable. I need to tell someone."

Kofi tried to grab his brother's arm. "No! Sefu, don't tell anyone yet! It's a secret!"

But Sefu was already running up the path toward the village, his curiosity and excitement too strong to keep silent. Kofi and Nia exchanged worried glances before turning to Almanza, who looked torn between worry and wonder.

"We should go after him," Nia said, glancing nervously at Almanza. "He might tell everyone."

The three hurried back, but by the time they reached the village square, Sefu was already speaking animatedly to his mother, who sat with Queen Adisa, sharing tea in a quiet corner under the shade of a large tree.

Sefu was breathless, his words spilling out in a jumble of excitement. "Mama, Queen Adisa! You won't believe what I saw—Almanza healed Red Bird's wing with her hands. Her eyes glowed, and the bird... it flew, like nothing had ever happened!"

Queen Adisa quickly set down her tea, her expression shifting to calm urgency. "Sefu," she said in a quiet but firm tone, "lower your voice. We do not want everyone hearing this story."

Sefu's mother, too, reached out and placed a gentle hand on his shoulder. "Hush now, Sefu. We need to speak of this quietly." She looked at the queen with worry and understanding, sensing the importance of keeping this matter private.

But it was too late; several nearby villagers had already caught Sefu's excited words and were glancing curiously in their direction, whispering amongst themselves. Word spread quickly, and soon, clusters of villagers exchanged hushed remarks, their faces alight with both wonder and unease.

Queen Adisa noticed the growing interest and gently motioned for Almanza to come to her. She wrapped an arm around Almanza's shoulders, a reassuring warmth that brought comfort to the child as she faced the many curious eyes.

One of the villagers, a woman named Amina, approached hesitantly. "Queen Adisa," she murmured, her eyes flickering to Almanza, "is it true? Has the child been gifted with... powers?"

Queen Adisa's gaze was calm and protective as she addressed Amina. "Almanza is a child of great spirit and kindness," she replied carefully, choosing her words with care. "She has a deep connection to the world around her, and her heart is filled with compassion. We should see this as a gift—a blessing upon our village."

The villagers murmured in awe, some nodding in agreement, while others exchanged wary glances. Sefu's mother placed a gentle hand on her son's shoulder, whispering to him, "You must be careful with your words, my child. Sometimes, gifts like this are best kept close to the heart."

Kofi and Nia stood close by Almanza's side, offering quiet support. Kofi gave his brother a small nudge, whispering, "Told you to keep it a secret..."

Sefu gave him a sheepish look, but he couldn't hide the admiration in his eyes. "I'm sorry. It was just... too amazing to keep quiet."

Almanza glanced up at the queen, her green eyes filled with questions, but Adisa simply smiled down at her with a look of unwavering trust and warmth. "Come, my child," she said, guiding Almanza gently. "Let us walk together, away from all these curious eyes."

As they walked away from the gathering, the queen's arm still around her shoulders, Almanza felt a deep sense of comfort and belonging, and in that moment, she knew that her power, whatever it might be, would be safe with Queen Adisa by her side.

*

CHAPTER SIX

The Healing Touch

THE VILLAGE WAS ALIVE with activity as the harvest season approached, and the air was filled with the earthy scent of ripening crops and the sounds of bustling preparation. Yet, amid the festive preparations and the general air of anticipation, a shadow had fallen over Maputo—a shadow that would test the true extent of Almanza's magical gifts.

It all began one crisp morning when the sun had just started to climb over the horizon. Adisa, as always, was awake before dawn, preparing for the day ahead. The palace grounds were quiet, save for the soft murmur of the early morning breeze rustling through the trees. Adisa had just finished her morning ritual when she received troubling news from one of the village elders, who had arrived at the palace in a state of concern.

"Your Majesty," Elder Osei said, his voice tinged with urgency, "there has been a terrible accident in the fields. One of our villagers, a farmer named Eba, has been gravely injured. His condition is worsening, and despite the efforts of our healers, he shows no sign of improvement. We fear for his life."

Adisa's heart sank at the news. Eba was a respected member of the community, known for his hard work and kindness. Without hesitation, Adisa resolved to visit Eba and see what could be done. As she prepared to leave, she turned to Almanza, who was playing quietly in the garden.

"Almanza," Adisa called gently, "I need you to come with me. We have a situation that requires your help."

Almanza looked up from her play, her eyes reflecting a mixture of curiosity and concern. She quickly joined her mother, her small hand finding Adisa's as they made their way to the scene of the accident.

The fields were bustling with activity as villagers gathered around the makeshift emergency area where Eba lay. The farmer was surrounded by a group of villagers and healers, his face pale and his breathing labored. The scene was chaotic, but Adisa's presence brought a semblance of order as she stepped forward.

Almanza, who had been watching from a distance, felt a surge of determination. She knew that this was a moment for her to step up and use her abilities to help. Adisa approached Eba's side, and Almanza followed, her heart pounding with both excitement and apprehension.

Elder Osei greeted them, his face lined with worry. "Your Majesty, Almanza, we've tried everything we know, but nothing seems to ease his pain or heal his injuries."

Adisa turned to Almanza, her eyes filled with both hope and caution. "Almanza, this is your opportunity to use your gifts. Remember what we've discussed—act with care and compassion."

Almanza nodded, her gaze steady and focused. She approached Eba's side, her heart aching at the sight of the suffering man. She knelt beside him, placing her hands gently over his wounds. Taking a deep breath, she closed her eyes and centered herself, drawing upon the knowledge and guidance she had received from Nana Eba and her mother.

With deliberate intent, Almanza began to channel her energy. She focused on the warmth of the sun and the life-giving forces of the earth, allowing her magic to flow through her hands and into Eba's body. A soft, golden light began to emanate from her fingertips, casting a soothing glow over the injured man.

As Almanza worked, she could feel the tension and pain in Eba's body gradually easing. The light grew brighter, and the air around her seemed to hum with a gentle, healing energy. The villagers watched in awe as Almanza's magic took effect, their expressions a mix of hope and amazement.

For a brief moment, it seemed as though the healing was working. Eba's breathing steadied, and his color began to return. The villagers sighed with relief, and Adisa's heart swelled with pride and gratitude. Almanza looked up at her mother, her face flushed with the effort but also glowing with satisfaction.

But as Almanza continued to concentrate, she began to feel an unfamiliar weariness settling over her. The magic that had once flowed so effortlessly now felt strained and heavy. The light around her dimmed, and Eba's condition, though improved, was far from fully restored.

Almanza's hands trembled slightly, and she could see the concern in the eyes of those around her. Elder Osei stepped forward, his voice filled with both encouragement and concern. "Almanza, you've done well, but you must take care of yourself as well. Healing is a delicate process."

Almanza took a deep breath, her energy waning. She pulled back her hands and looked at Eba, who was now stable but still in need of further care. Adisa placed a reassuring hand on her daughter's shoulder.

"You did your best, Almanza," Adisa said gently. "You have made a significant difference. We will continue to care for Eba and ensure that he receives the help he needs."

Almanza nodded, feeling a mixture of relief and exhaustion. As the villagers continued to attend to Eba, Adisa guided Almanza away from the scene, leading her back to the palace. The journey was quiet, and Almanza's thoughts were consumed by the experience.

When they reached the palace, Adisa led Almanza to her private chamber and helped her settle into a comfortable seat. She fetched a bowl of cool water and some restorative herbs, knowing that Almanza would need to regain her strength after such an intense exertion of magic.

As Almanza sipped the water, Adisa sat beside her, her expression thoughtful. "Almanza, you did something truly remarkable today. Your healing brought hope and relief to Eba and the villagers. But it's important to remember that magic can be draining, and its effects are not always immediate or perfect."

Almanza looked up, her eyes filled with concern. "Mama, was there something I did wrong? Why didn't the healing work completely?"

Adisa shook her head, her voice gentle. "No, Almanza, you didn't do anything wrong. Healing is a complex process, and sometimes it takes more time than we expect. Your magic is powerful, but it is also finite. You must learn to balance your energy and recognize when you need to rest."

Almanza nodded, absorbing her mother's words. "I understand, Mama. I just wanted to help as much as I could."

Adisa smiled, placing a comforting hand on her daughter's. "And you did help. Your efforts made a difference, and that is something to be proud of. But remember, it's also important to listen to your own body and take care of yourself. Magic is a tool, and it must be used wisely and with respect."

As the sun dipped below the horizon and the evening shadows lengthened, Almanza rested, her mother's words echoing in her mind. She had learned a valuable lesson about the limitations and responsibilities that came with her powers. The experience had been both exhilarating and humbling, a reminder of the delicate balance required in the practice of magic.

In the days that followed, Eba's condition continued to improve, and the villagers expressed their gratitude to Almanza for her assistance. Though the healing was not complete, the progress made was a testament to the power of her gifts and the potential for future success.

Almanza remained committed to honing her abilities and learning more about the nuances of magic. She continued to work closely with her mother and the village healers, seeking to understand the deeper aspects of her gifts and how to use them effectively.

Adisa watched with pride as her daughter grew into her role as a healer and protector of the village. The lessons of caution and balance remained at the forefront of Almanza's mind, guiding her actions and decisions. The journey of mastering her abilities was just beginning, and with each step, Almanza moved closer to fulfilling her potential and making a lasting impact on the world around her.

As Almanza lay resting in her mother's chamber, the reality of her healing powers settled over her like a weight. She had felt so connected to Eba's pain, so certain she could relieve him entirely, yet her magic had reached its limits. She looked to Queen Adisa with questioning eyes.

"Mama, if I was meant to heal, why did my strength falter?" she asked quietly. "Why was I only able to ease his pain but not restore him fully?"

Queen Adisa sighed, leaning closer. "Almanza, sometimes even the purest intentions cannot alter what is beyond our control. There are forces greater than us, and we must learn humility before them. Healing, my dear, is a gift but not a guarantee."

Almanza frowned. "But Mama, I felt something deep inside urging me to help him. I thought my magic was enough if I wanted to save him. Wasn't I created with this gift by God? Didn't God want me to use it to save a life?"

Queen Adisa's expression grew stern, and her voice became steady and clear. "Yes, Almanza, you were given this gift by God, and it is a blessing. But understand this: life and death do not belong to you or to me. The power to heal is not the same as the power to decide who lives or dies. That choice belongs to God alone."

Almanza's young face was a mixture of defiance and hurt. "If God gave me this ability, who's to say it isn't meant to be used whenever I feel it's right? How can I know when it's truly God's will?"

Adisa saw her daughter's frustration rising, the intensity in her green eyes sparking. She took a breath, her own heart tightening as she chose her next words. "Since we are not God, Almanza, we will never truly know. And that is exactly why we must tread carefully." Her voice was firm, but not unkind.

Frustrated, Almanza stared down at her hands, feeling both the weight and limitation of her powers. Before she could respond, Queen Adisa rose, her expression unreadable as she spoke quietly. "Think on this, Almanza. Our powers do not make us gods, nor should we pretend they do." And with a steady step, she turned and left the chamber, leaving Almanza alone with her thoughts.

The silence that followed felt heavy. Almanza's emotions flared, and unable to contain them, she stood and rushed out of the palace, her feet carrying her to the forest beyond Maputo's borders, where she trained daily under the watchful eye of Nana Suma.

In the forest, surrounded by towering trees and the soft rustle of leaves, Almanza felt herself begin to calm. The woods had always been a place of refuge for her—a world of quiet, of mystery, where she could connect with her powers and herself. She felt the familiar presence of Nana Suma before she even saw her, the elder woman standing by a grove of trees, her eyes wise and knowing.

Nana Suma looked at Almanza, her gaze both gentle and piercing. "You are troubled, child."

Almanza nodded, her fists clenched. "I don't understand, Nana. Why did my mother react like that? I only wanted to help Eba, to heal him. Isn't that what my powers are for?"

Nana Suma motioned for Almanza to sit on a fallen log, settling beside her as she spoke. "Your mother is wise, Almanza. She wants you to understand that with great power comes an even greater responsibility. To use your powers effectively, you must first learn restraint and understand that sometimes, even when we want to intervene, it is not our place."

Almanza's eyes flashed with frustration. "But I could feel it, Nana. I could feel the strength within me, and yet it was like something held me back."

"Perhaps something was," Nana Suma replied softly. "Not every illness or injury is meant to be cured by your hand. There is a balance to the world, and sometimes, fate must take its course."

The young girl looked down, her voice barely a whisper. "But what if I could have done more?"

Nana Suma placed a comforting hand on Almanza's shoulder. "You did everything you could, and you brought Eba great relief. But you must understand, Almanza—magic has limits, and so do we. If you try to carry the weight of every life, it will crush you. You must learn to accept your limits and find peace within them."

Almanza nodded slowly, absorbing her mentor's words, even as questions continued to swirl in her mind. Nana Suma studied her face thoughtfully before speaking again.

"There is another lesson for you to learn here," she said. "Today, your magic was a gift, but I have seen it flare in ways that were... more intense, shall we say."

Almanza's expression turned curious, then apprehensive. "What do you mean?"

Nana Suma's gaze was steady. "I have noticed that your powers surge when you are calm and focused, but they become wild and unpredictable when you are upset. Do you remember the time you had a small argument with Kofi, and we had a storm over the village for three days?"

Almanza's eyes widened as she remembered, her voice barely a whisper. "That was me?"

"Yes, child," Nana Suma replied, her voice firm. "You do not yet understand the extent of your abilities. I even heard from others that the lightning seemed to emerge from your very hands. That storm was your anger, unleashed."

Almanza's heart pounded as the realization sank in. "I didn't mean to do that..."

Nana Suma's voice softened. "I know. You have a good heart, Almanza, but goodness alone cannot always control power. It takes discipline and training. You must learn to master yourself if you are to master your gift."

Almanza's gaze grew determined. "Then I will train harder. I will learn to control my powers."

Nana Suma placed a hand on Almanza's shoulder, meeting her eyes. "There is more, child. It is not only about control. You must train as a warrior."

Almanza blinked in surprise. "A warrior? But... my mother wants me to be a healer, a protector."

"Those roles are not so different," Nana Suma said with a small smile. "Healers are protectors, yes, but warriors protect as well. One day, someone will come to challenge your right to lead, to challenge your place here. It is no secret to some that you were not born into this bloodline, and there are those who will not accept your right to rule unless you can defend it."

Almanza felt a pang of hurt and confusion. "But... my mother chose me. I am her daughter. Does that not make me part of the royal family?"

Nana Suma gave her a gentle but knowing look. "To your mother, yes. To me, yes. To those who love and know you, you are our future queen. But to others, to those who do not know your heart, you may be seen as an outsider. And those who seek power will use any reason they can to test your right to lead."

Almanza's expression hardened, a spark of resolve igniting within her. "Then I will become strong enough that no one will dare challenge me."

Nana Suma smiled approvingly. "That is the spirit of a leader. But remember, strength comes not only from the magic within you but from discipline, wisdom, and the courage to make difficult choices. You must learn to be a leader who commands respect and a warrior who can protect."

Almanza nodded, her gaze fierce and unyielding. "I will train, Nana. I will be ready."

As the moon rose above the forest, casting a silver glow over the trees, Almanza felt a sense of purpose settle within her. Her path was beginning to unfold, filled with challenges and responsibilities she had yet to fully comprehend. But with Nana Suma's guidance and her mother's love, she was ready to face whatever lay ahead.

Together, Almanza and Nana Suma began their first lesson in the art of combat, the sounds of their movements blending with the whispers of the forest, as if nature itself was bearing witness to the growth of Maputo's future queen.

CHAPTER SEVEN

A Mother's Warning

THE MORNING SUN CAST a golden hue over the village of Maputo, its rays filtering through the trees and illuminating the palace in a warm glow. Queen Adisa stood by her window, deep in thought, watching as the village came alive with the hustle and bustle of a new day. She knew that today would be a day of significance. Almanza, her beloved daughter, was growing rapidly, her powers blossoming in ways that both awed and concerned Adisa. She had known from the start that Almanza was special, but with each passing year, her abilities became more pronounced, drawing admiration—and a touch of fear—from the villagers.

Inside her private chamber, surrounded by symbols of her lineage and family, Adisa took a deep breath. She had raised Almanza with boundless love, guiding her gently through life's mysteries. But as her daughter's powers grew, so did the weight of responsibility that rested upon Adisa's shoulders. Today, she would speak with Almanza about the importance of caution, wisdom, and self-restraint, qualities essential for one who held such gifts.

She sent for Almanza, who came quickly, her bright green eyes brimming with curiosity and excitement. Almanza was a picture of vibrancy, her energy as boundless as the wind, yet as gentle as the morning dew. The queen's heart swelled with pride as she looked at her daughter, knowing that the child before her was a gift, a precious balance of light and power.

"Come in, my dear," Adisa said, patting the seat beside her with a warm smile. "I've been meaning to talk to you about something very important."

Almanza's eyes sparkled with anticipation as she sat beside her mother, her hands folded in her lap. "Is it about my powers, Mama?"

Adisa nodded, her smile softening. "Yes, my child. You have grown so much, and with each day, I see your powers becoming stronger and more beautiful. The villagers admire you, and they have come to respect your gifts. But with these gifts come responsibilities and, sometimes, burdens."

Almanza looked up, her brow furrowed slightly. "Burdens? I don't understand, Mama. I only want to help people and make them happy."

Adisa reached over, placing a gentle hand on Almanza's shoulder. "I know, my dear. Your heart is pure, and your intentions are good. But magic, especially the kind you possess, must be used with great care. You see, each time we use our power, there is an effect—an impact on the world around us. And if we're not careful, even well-meant actions can bring about unintended consequences."

Almanza nodded slowly, her expression thoughtful. "How do I know when it's right to use my powers, then?"

Adisa's gaze softened, and she chose her words carefully. "It starts with understanding your intentions, Almanza. Always ask yourself why you're using your magic. Think about who it will help and who it might harm, even unintentionally. Remember, magic is a gift from the Creator, and it is our responsibility to use it wisely, not for personal gain or to show off, but only when it is truly needed."

Almanza's eyes drifted to the intricate charms adorning her mother's wrist, their symbols a reminder of the wisdom passed down through generations. "I understand, Mama. I will be careful."

A moment of silence settled between them as Almanza absorbed her mother's words. Then, Adisa continued, her tone more serious. "There is something else, Almanza. Not everyone understands the power you have. Some may see it as a blessing, but others may see it as something to fear. There are those in this world who might try to use you for their own purposes or turn the village against you out of fear."

Almanza's gaze dropped to the floor, her small fingers twisting in her lap. She had always felt safe and loved in Maputo, but the thought of being feared or misunderstood unsettled her. "But why would anyone be afraid of me, Mama?"

Adisa sighed, a look of sadness crossing her face. "People often fear what they do not understand. You are a light in this village, Almanza, but even a light can cast shadows. It is up to you to be mindful of how you use your powers and to keep yourself grounded in kindness and humility. Do you understand?"

Almanza nodded slowly, her expression somber. "I will try, Mama. But... what if I make a mistake?"

Adisa smiled gently, her hand brushing Almanza's cheek. "Mistakes are part of learning, my child. What matters is that you learn from them and continue to grow. And remember, you are not alone in this journey. I am here, and so is the wisdom of our ancestors."

She reached into a nearby drawer and pulled out a small, ornate box, carefully opening it to reveal a shimmering green amulet adorned with delicate symbols of protection and guidance. She handed it to Almanza, who accepted it with reverence.

"This amulet belonged to my grandmother," Adisa said softly. "It is meant to protect and focus magical energy. I want you to keep it with you. Let it serve as a reminder to approach your powers with caution and respect."

Almanza looked at the amulet, her eyes wide with awe as she traced the symbols with her fingers. "Thank you, Mama. I will carry it with me always."

Adisa wrapped her arms around her daughter, her heart filled with both pride and a flicker of apprehension. "You have a kind heart and a strong spirit, Almanza. You will do great things, but remember, with each power comes a choice. Choose wisely, my dear."

As they held each other, Adisa's voice softened, a mixture of pride and motherly protectiveness. "You have the potential to bring so much light to this world, Almanza. But to protect that light, you must also learn to protect yourself. You will train to be strong, not only in heart and mind but in body as well. This power of yours is a blessing, but it is also something you must guard carefully."

Almanza looked up, curiosity mingling with determination. "I will be strong, Mama. For our village... and for you."

In the hours that followed, Almanza wandered the village, contemplating her mother's words. She felt the weight of the amulet against her chest, a reminder of her responsibility and her duty. As she passed by the fields, she saw villagers going about their daily work, their faces etched with contentment as they shared stories and laughter. The people of Maputo were kind and hardworking, and Almanza felt a renewed sense of purpose—to use her powers to protect them, but to do so wisely.

As she walked, she noticed an elderly villager struggling to carry a heavy bundle of firewood. Her instincts urged her to reach out, to use her magic to lighten the load, but she remembered her mother's words about understanding the consequences of each action. Instead, Almanza walked up to the villager and offered her hands, taking some of the load and carrying it alongside her with a smile.

The old woman beamed at Almanza. "Thank you, my child. You are a blessing to this village."

Almanza nodded, her heart swelling with pride and understanding. Sometimes, strength was not in the magic itself but in the choice to act with kindness and humility.

Later that evening, Queen Adisa stood alone in her chambers, looking out over the village bathed in the warm glow of dusk. The air was still, and a sense of calm settled over her as she watched her people wind down from the day's work. She could see Almanza in the distance, laughing with Nia and Kofi, her green eyes bright with innocence and wonder.

As she gazed at her daughter, Adisa felt the familiar tug of worry, but she also felt hope—a hope that Almanza would carry her legacy forward, that she would become not only a powerful force but a wise and compassionate leader. In that moment, she sent a silent prayer to the ancestors, asking for their guidance and protection for the child who had become her own.

"You will be strong, my daughter," she whispered softly, "and you will be wise. The path may not always be easy, but know that you are loved, always."

And as the stars began to appear in the sky, Adisa felt a sense of peace, knowing that she had planted the seeds of wisdom and strength in her daughter's heart, trusting that they would grow and flourish in the days to come.

As night fully settled over Maputo, Almanza returned home, her mind brimming with thoughts about her mother's words. She slipped into bed, clutching the amulet Queen Adisa had given her, feeling the smooth, cool weight of it in her hand. As she drifted off to sleep, her mind echoed with her mother's wisdom—magic is a gift, but one that must be used with caution and understanding.

In her dreams, Almanza found herself in a vast, open field, surrounded by towering trees with leaves that glowed softly in the darkness. The air hummed with life, and she could feel a warm, gentle presence around her, as if the very earth itself was watching over her. She looked down at her hands, which were faintly glowing with the same green light she'd seen in her eyes when she healed Red Bird. She felt strong and connected, as though the world around her was a part of her, and she of it.

In her dream, a voice—soft yet powerful—whispered, "Remember, little one, your heart is your guide. Magic answers to it. Keep it pure, and your path will be clear."

When Almanza awoke, the first light of dawn was seeping through her window, casting a warm glow across her room. The amulet still lay in her hand, its presence grounding her. She held it tightly, feeling the weight of the responsibility her mother had entrusted her with. Rising from her bed, she dressed quietly, deciding that today, she would visit the village and learn from her mother's teachings, practicing kindness and humility in small, simple ways.

The villagers had already started their morning tasks when Almanza walked through the village. She stopped to help an elder, refilled water jugs for families, and gathered herbs for Nana Suma, each act simple but deliberate. With each small task, she remembered her mother's words, thinking carefully before offering her aid. Magic was powerful, but so was kindness, she realized.

As the day wore on, she noticed a small gathering of children by the edge of the village. They were crowded around a tree, pointing and talking excitedly. Almanza walked over, curious to see what had captured their attention.

In the branches of the tree, perched with a quiet dignity, was Red Bird. Her wings shimmered faintly with a glow Almanza recognized, a reminder of the healing touch she'd given her friend. The children watched in awe as Red Bird turned her head and gazed directly at Almanza, as if acknowledging the connection they shared.

One of the children, a little girl named Miri, looked up at Almanza with wide eyes. "Almanza, you helped Red Bird, didn't you? She looks even more beautiful now!"

Almanza smiled, feeling a warmth in her heart. "Yes, I did. But Red Bird was strong all on her own. I only helped a little."

Miri's eyes sparkled with admiration. "I want to be like you, Almanza! You're so kind and brave."

Almanza knelt down, meeting Miri's gaze. "Being kind and brave doesn't require magic, Miri. You have that in you already. Just remember to always think of others and listen to your heart."

Miri nodded enthusiastically, and the other children murmured in agreement, inspired by Almanza's words. As they dispersed, Almanza felt a sense of pride and calm, knowing she was using her gifts and her mother's guidance wisely.

That evening, as Adisa watched Almanza interact with the villagers, she felt her heart swell with pride. Almanza moved with a gentle grace, her compassion and maturity beyond her years. Adisa could see the wisdom and restraint growing within her daughter, a reflection of the lessons she had imparted. Yet, Adisa knew that these small acts of kindness and self-control were only the beginning.

Almanza's powers would continue to grow, and there would come a day when she would face true tests, challenges that would call on her to use her magic in ways that even Adisa could not predict. For now, though, Adisa was content to watch her daughter flourish, guiding her with a gentle hand and a loving heart.

Later, as the two sat together by the fire, Adisa spoke softly, her voice filled with hope and a tinge of sorrow. "One day, Almanza, you may face a time when you'll have to make difficult choices alone. You'll know the weight of protecting others, of guiding them, even when they don't understand your gifts. But remember, your heart is your compass. Keep it steady and true."

Almanza listened intently, her young face serious and thoughtful. She nodded, absorbing her mother's words. "I will, Mama. I promise to remember your advice and use my powers wisely."

Adisa reached out, pulling Almanza into a warm embrace. "You're strong, my child, and I am proud of you every day. Know that I will always be with you, in your heart and in spirit, guiding you."

They stayed by the fire until the flames died down, Adisa's arms wrapped protectively around her daughter. For Adisa, this quiet moment was a reminder of the precious time they had together, and a silent prayer that Almanza would continue to grow into the leader she was destined to be.

Together, they gazed into the last embers, each of them silently reflecting on the journey that lay ahead, knowing that the bond they shared would carry them through whatever trials the future held. And as the village settled into the calm of the night, Adisa felt a profound sense of peace, knowing that she had planted the seeds of wisdom, love, and courage in Almanza's heart—gifts that would guide her daughter through the mysteries of her powers and beyond.

As the night deepened, Queen Adisa summoned Nana Suma to her chambers. The elder, with her deep-set eyes that seemed to hold the knowledge of generations, arrived quietly, her presence both calming and powerful. Adisa motioned for her to sit by the fire, her face thoughtful as she prepared herself to discuss her daughter's future.

Once settled, Nana Suma looked directly at the queen, her voice soft but firm. "Queen Adisa, it is time. The child must be trained."

Adisa's brow furrowed. "Trained? She is so young, Suma. She barely understands the full extent of her abilities. I worry that placing such responsibility on her shoulders too soon could burden her."

Nana Suma nodded slowly, her expression sympathetic but resolute. "I understand, my queen, but Almanza's powers grow quickly. And while you have guided her well, there is a depth to her magic that must be channeled, for her safety as well as ours. Her heart is pure, yes, but her powers have already begun to ripple through Maputo—and beyond."

Adisa's face fell, concern clouding her eyes. "Do you mean... the villagers know more than I thought?"

Nana Suma met her gaze, her eyes holding a quiet gravity. "More than you might realize. They speak in hushed voices about Almanza's gift. They tell stories of how Red Bird was healed, but that is not all. There were small moments, brief uses of her magic that she may not even have noticed herself, yet they were seen."

Adisa took a sharp breath, her worry deepening. "What else have they seen?"

"Little things," Nana Suma replied. "A wilting flower that blossomed again with her touch, a storm that softened when she stood beneath it, a calf that recovered from an injury within hours after Almanza touched it. They may seem like innocent gestures, but they leave their mark, and the villagers have begun to notice. Some are in awe of her, yes, but others... they whisper of things they do not understand."

Adisa clasped her hands together, her fingers tightening as she considered the elder's words. "I tried to shield her, to guide her quietly so she could grow in peace, without fear or suspicion. But you are right—Almanza's light shines too brightly to be hidden."

Nana Suma nodded, her voice gentle but firm. "The villagers of Maputo may respect you, my queen, but even respect cannot always silence fear. And if this fear grows, it will spread, as it already has begun to do. Word has reached the nearby villages, and it will not be long before they come seeking the truth. Some may come out of curiosity, others out of admiration, but a few... may come with ill intent."

Adisa's face grew pale as she absorbed the weight of Nana Suma's warning. "You think someone may come to harm her?"

Nana Suma's gaze was steady, her expression solemn. "I do not know who or when, but I know this: powers as rare as Almanza's are often desired by those who would wield them for their own purposes. Magic has a way of attracting both light and shadow. If word continues to spread, we may face those who wish to claim her abilities, whether by persuasion or force."

Adisa's hands clenched tightly, her voice low with determination. "No one will take her from me. I will protect her with my life if I must."

Nana Suma reached out, placing a calming hand on Adisa's arm. "And that is why we must act now. You have guarded her well, but it is time to teach Almanza to guard herself. She must understand the nature of her powers, their strengths and limitations. If she is to carry this gift, she must know how to wield it with both courage and restraint."

Adisa took a deep breath, the tension in her shoulders slowly easing. "How, Suma? How can I train her when I myself do not fully understand what lies within her?"

Nana Suma's eyes softened with understanding. "You will not be alone, my queen. There are rituals, ancient practices that can guide her. I will help in whatever ways I can, and I will teach you both. But Almanza must learn to focus, to control her magic, and to protect herself against those who might seek to take advantage of her gift."

Adisa nodded, her face resolute but tinged with sadness. "I wanted her to grow up free, without the burdens that accompany power. I wanted her to have a childhood of joy and innocence..."

Nana Suma's hand tightened on Adisa's arm, her voice filled with compassion. "Almanza's spirit is joyful, and that joy will remain, no matter the training. But her path is unique, my queen. If we guide her now, she will grow to be both wise and strong. She will learn to use her powers for the good of all and to protect herself from those who may seek to harm her."

Adisa looked into the fire, the flames casting a warm glow over her face as she considered the path ahead. She glanced back at Nana Suma, her voice filled with gratitude and determination. "Then we shall begin. Almanza will be prepared for whatever may come. She is my daughter, and I will see that she is ready to face the world, with all its wonder and dangers."

Nana Suma smiled, her face etched with both pride and hope. "With your love and guidance, Queen Adisa, Almanza will be a force of light in this world, and her strength will be a beacon for all who call Maputo home."

And as the two women sat together, their hearts united in purpose, they knew that Almanza's journey had truly begun.

Nana Suma observed the deepening concern etched on Queen Adisa's face and leaned forward, her voice dropping to a softer, more serious tone. "There is something else, my queen. I have noticed something about Almanza's powers—something that troubles me."

Adisa looked up sharply, her gaze focused, tension building in her frame. "What is it, Suma? Speak plainly."

Nana Suma took a breath, choosing her words carefully. "Almanza's powers are not only strong but... intense, especially when her emotions are stirred. She is a well-tempered child, yes, but as she grows, her heart will know anger, and in those moments, her powers will be difficult to control."

Adisa's eyes darkened as memories surfaced. She had seen small flashes of Almanza's strength during moments of frustration—nothing drastic, but enough to make her aware of the fire her daughter carried within. "I have seen it, Suma. When she is upset, it's as if the earth itself responds to her."

Nana Suma nodded. "Once, when Almanza was angered by a small argument with one of the children, the village was cast into a storm for three days. The skies churned with her anger, rain pouring without pause, and lightning split the sky as if commanded by her hand. It is no small gift, Adisa. We must recognize the potential danger."

Queen Adisa's jaw tightened as she processed this. "Almanza has always been gentle. She does not provoke easily."

"But emotions, my queen, are like the wind. They can be soft one moment and fierce the next," Nana Suma continued. "As she grows, her heart will know new depths, and she must learn to control herself even in those times. Anger, grief, fear—if they spark her powers before she has learned to channel them, the consequences could be grave."

Adisa lowered her gaze, struggling to reconcile her love for Almanza's innocent spirit with the realization that her child held a power that could both save and destroy. Nana

Suma placed a hand on Adisa's arm, her eyes filled with compassion.

"Almanza must learn more than just restraint, my queen. She must learn to protect herself. She must train as a warrior."

Adisa's eyes flickered with alarm. "A warrior?"

"Yes," Nana Suma said firmly. "Her magic alone will not be enough. One day, someone will challenge her bloodline. We must prepare her to defend herself and, more importantly, to defend Maputo. She may not be of royal blood, but if she is to rule, she will need to hold her place by right and by strength."

At the mention of Almanza's bloodline, Adisa's face tightened. "She is of royal blood, Suma. Her bloodline is mine. I have made her my daughter, and she is as much a part of this family as any who have come before."

Nana Suma bowed her head respectfully, but her gaze was steady as she replied. "I know, my queen. And no one doubts your love or the bond you share. But others outside of Maputo may see her origins as an opportunity to challenge her legitimacy."

Adisa's jaw clenched, her voice steely. "How dare you speak of her this way? I have raised Almanza as my own, and she will be queen. Her heritage does not lessen her worth."

Nana Suma's voice softened. "Forgive me, Adisa. You know I speak only out of concern. You are a strong leader—one of the strongest Maputo has known—and you have proven yourself time and again. But there are those beyond our borders who would test her strength simply because of where she came from."

The queen's gaze fell, her expression clouded by memories of pain and loss. She had fought hard to maintain Maputo's peace, to shield her people from the devastation of war. She had lost her brother, her husband, and her only child in a brutal conflict between two rival villages, a tragedy that had left her heart scarred but had forged her into a ruler who would not be easily challenged.

Her family had been caught in the crossfire during a time of peace, on what should have been a simple hunting and training excursion in the neighboring village. But as they traveled back to Maputo, they were ambushed. Adisa's brother, a warrior who had served her faithfully, was killed alongside her husband and child. She was left alone, yet she had not wavered, standing tall to lead Maputo with an unbreakable resolve.

Adisa, known for her beauty and grace, had gained respect not just for her appearance but for her fierce strength and wisdom. She was a queen who ruled not out of tradition but out of capability. She had held Maputo together with her resilience, guiding her people through loss and prosperity alike. And although her heart had found solace in Almanza, the child she had taken in, she knew that the time would come when that same child would need to defend her own place.

Taking a deep breath, Adisa looked at Nana Suma, her voice steadier now but laced with sadness. "I understand, Suma. You are right. Almanza will one day face challenges I may not be here to protect her from. And it pains me to think of it... but she must be prepared. She must learn to be strong, not just in heart and magic, but in body and skill."

Nana Suma nodded approvingly. "Then let us begin her training, my queen. She must learn to harness her power, to understand its depth and breadth. But she must also learn the discipline of combat, the strength that lies in both the mind and body."

Adisa's voice softened, her heart torn between a mother's love and a ruler's duty. "I wanted her to remain a child for as long as possible. I wanted her to know peace and joy, unburdened by the weight of power and the fear that comes with it."

Nana Suma placed a hand over Adisa's, her expression understanding. "You have given her that gift, Adisa, and it will always be a part of her. But now she must grow into the woman she was meant to be. She has a rare gift, and with it comes a destiny greater than most. Let us help her walk that path with confidence and strength."

Adisa looked toward the window, where the stars were just beginning to appear, casting their soft light over Maputo. Her mind filled with visions of Almanza—innocent and joyful, yet carrying within her the power to change the fate of their village. She knew that she could not hold her daughter back, that the time had come to let her begin the journey that awaited her.

"Very well, Suma," she said, her voice resolute. "We will prepare Almanza for what lies ahead. She will train as a warrior, as a leader. And when the time comes, she will be ready to face any who dare to challenge her or her place among us."

Nana Suma smiled, relief and respect evident in her gaze. "Thank you, my queen. Together, we will make sure that Almanza's light is a beacon of hope and strength for Maputo. She will become not only the queen this village needs, but a force that even our enemies will hesitate to face."

Adisa reached out, clasping Nana Suma's hands in a rare display of vulnerability. "I cannot do this alone, Suma. She is my heart, my reason for hope. I have lost so much already... I cannot bear to lose her."

Nana Suma's gaze softened, and she placed a comforting hand over Adisa's. "You will not lose her, Adisa. Almanza is strong, and she has you to guide her. Together, we will help her grow into the ruler she was meant to be."

Adisa nodded, a quiet strength returning to her eyes. She looked out into the night, a silent promise forming in her heart. No harm shall come to Almanza. She will know both the love of her people and the strength to protect them.

And as the stars shone brightly over Maputo, the queen and the elder sat together, their hearts united in a shared purpose, ready to face the journey that would prepare Almanza for the path destiny had set before her.

Chapter Eight

The Rumors Begin

THE DAY WAS LONG dictated the flow of daily activities, change was often met with a mixture of curiosity and skepticism. The arrival of the harvest season had brought a sense of excitement and anticipation, but it also brought with it an undercurrent of unease—an unease centered around the young girl with the extraordinary green eyes, Almanza.

The events of the past weeks had left a deep impression on the village. Almanza's act of healing Eba had demonstrated the incredible power of her magic, but it had also sown seeds of doubt and apprehension among some of the villagers. As word of her abilities spread, whispers began to circulate, and the once harmonious atmosphere of Maputo began to shift.

One warm afternoon, as the villagers went about their daily tasks, a group of women gathered near the communal well. Their conversation, initially focused on the harvest and preparations for the upcoming festival, had subtly shifted to the subject of Almanza.

"Have you heard," said Esi, a middle-aged woman known for her sharp wit, "about the girl with the green eyes? They say she has the power to heal with a touch."

"Yes," replied Ama, another villager, her voice laced with a hint of unease. "I saw it with my own eyes. She helped Eba, but not completely. He's still ill, despite her magic."

"Magic can be unpredictable," Esi continued, her tone contemplative. "It's not always what it seems. I've heard stories of magic that brought more trouble than it was worth."

The murmurs of agreement and skepticism grew louder, and the conversation quickly became the focus of the village's chatter. Some villagers expressed admiration for Almanza's abilities, seeing her as a source of hope and a symbol of the village's resilience. Others, however, viewed her powers with suspicion, worried about the potential consequences and the unknowns that came with magic.

At the heart of this growing unease was a sense of fear of the unknown. Magic was a force deeply intertwined with the traditions and beliefs of Maputo, but it was also something that few truly understood. The fear of what might happen if Almanza's powers went awry or if her abilities were misused began to overshadow the initial awe and gratitude that had greeted her healing.

In the palace, Queen Adisa was acutely aware of the shift in the village's mood. The once jubilant celebrations and expressions of thanks had given way to whispers and sidelong glances. Adisa knew that her daughter's powers, while a source of great potential, also carried with them a weighty responsibility and the risk of misinterpretation.

One evening, as Adisa and Almanza were sharing a quiet meal together, the topic of the growing rumors came up. Almanza, who had been keenly observant of the changing atmosphere, asked her mother about the whispers she had heard.

"Mother," Almanza began, her voice tinged with concern, "why are people starting to talk about me in such a way? I thought they were happy with what I did for Eba."

Adisa set her cup down and looked at her daughter with a mixture of sadness and resolve. "Almanza, whenever something new or unusual occurs, especially something as powerful as magic, people react in different ways. Some are eager to understand and embrace it, while others fear what they do not know."

"But why would they fear me?" Almanza asked, her eyes wide with confusion. "I only wanted to help."

Adisa reached across the table and took Almanza's hand in her own. "It's not about you personally, my dear. It's about the uncertainty that comes with something as profound as magic. People fear what they don't understand, and they worry about what might happen if things go wrong."

Almanza sighed, her heart heavy with the weight of her mother's words. "What should I do?"

Adisa offered a comforting smile. "Continue to act with kindness and integrity. Show the villagers that your intentions are pure and that you are dedicated to using your powers for the good of the community. Over time, they will come to see that your gifts are a blessing, not a threat."

As the days went by, the village's response to Almanza's magic remained a mixture of fascination and trepidation. The ongoing whispers and rumors began to take on a life of their own, fueled by a series of unexplained incidents and the natural tendency of people to seek explanations for the unknown.

One morning, as Almanza was practicing her healing techniques in the palace garden, she overheard a conversation between two villagers passing by the palace gates. Their words, though hushed, were filled with concern.

"They say she's not just healing the sick," one of them said. "Some think she might be controlling the weather or causing misfortune."

"That's just talk," the other replied. "But there are signs that something strange is happening. Crops in certain fields aren't growing as well as they used to."

Almanza's heart sank as she listened to the exchange. She knew that she had no control over the weather or the growth of crops, but the rumors seemed to be gaining traction, creating a sense of fear and unease among the villagers.

As she pondered the situation, Almanza realized that she needed to address the concerns directly. With her mother's guidance, she decided to organize a community meeting to address the rumors and reassure the villagers about her intentions.

Adisa supported Almanza's decision, understanding the importance of open communication and transparency. The meeting was scheduled for the following week, and word quickly spread throughout the village. The event was met with a mix of curiosity and apprehension, as the villagers prepared to hear directly from the girl who had become the center of so much speculation.

On the day of the meeting, the village square was filled with a gathering of villagers, their expressions reflecting a range of emotions from hope to skepticism. Adisa and Almanza stood at the front of the crowd, the Queen's regal presence providing a sense of authority and stability.

As the crowd settled, Almanza stepped forward, her heart racing but her resolve firm. She looked out at the faces before her, each one reflecting a different facet of the village's collective anxiety.

"Thank you all for coming," Almanza began, her voice steady but filled with emotion. "I know that there have been many rumors and concerns about my abilities, and I want to address them directly. My intention in using my magic has always been to help and support our community, not to cause harm or create fear."

She paused, allowing her words to resonate. "I understand that magic can be a mysterious and sometimes unsettling force. But I want you to know that I am committed to using my gifts responsibly. I have been learning from my mother and the village healers, and I am dedicated to ensuring that my actions are guided by compassion and respect for our traditions."

Almanza's words were met with a mix of nods and murmurs from the crowd. Some villagers seemed reassured by her sincerity, while others remained wary. Adisa stepped forward to offer her support, her voice filled with warmth and authority.

"Almanza has shown great care and dedication in her efforts to assist those in need," Adisa said. "We must remember that new things can be intimidating, but it is our duty to approach them with open minds and hearts. We are a community that values understanding and support, and we should extend that to Almanza and her gifts."

The meeting continued with a discussion of how the village could support Almanza and address any concerns that arose. The dialogue was open and respectful, and while not all doubts were dispelled, there was a growing sense of willingness to give Almanza the benefit of the doubt.

As the crowd began to disperse, Almanza and Adisa shared a quiet moment of reflection. The meeting had been a step towards bridging the gap between fear and understanding, but there was still work to be done.

"You did well, Almanza," Adisa said, her voice filled with pride. "You faced the rumors with courage and honesty. It will take time, but with continued effort and transparency, the villagers will come to see the value of your gifts."

Almanza nodded, her heart lighter despite the lingering uncertainty. "Thank you, Mama. I'll keep doing my best and showing them that my magic is meant for good."

As the sun set over Maputo, casting long shadows across the village, Almanza knew that her journey was far from over. The road to acceptance and understanding would be a long one, but with her mother's guidance and the support of those who believed in her, she was determined to navigate it with grace and perseverance.

The rumors and suspicion that had surrounded her were a reminder of the challenges that came with her extraordinary gifts. But they were also an opportunity to demonstrate the true nature of her magic and to prove that even in the face of fear, hope and compassion could prevail. The story of Almanza's journey was still unfolding, and with each step, she moved closer to a future where her powers would be embraced and celebrated as a force for good.

As the whispers in Maputo grew louder, the life Almanza had known began to shift. What had once been friendly smiles and warm greetings now turned into wary glances and hushed conversations. She felt the change keenly, like a chilly wind on a warm day, stinging and unwelcome. Her powers, once a source of pride, had now drawn an uncomfortable spotlight that cast her as both a miracle and a mystery.

To ground her, Queen Adisa continued to allow Almanza to attend school and training with her two best friends, Nia and Kofi. Adisa believed that Almanza needed to feel connected to her community, and her friendship with Nia and Kofi provided her with a refuge from the rumors. Yet, even among her peers, Almanza was not immune to the cruelty that sometimes came with fear.

One day, as the sun cast its warm light over the school grounds, Almanza made her way to the garden behind the school huts, where she often sought a quiet moment to herself. She had barely settled when a familiar voice echoed through the clearing.

"Well, well, if it isn't the queen's magical daughter," sneered a voice she recognized. It was Tafari, the meanest child in the village, flanked by a group of other children who had recently grown distant from her.

Almanza looked up, her heart sinking as Tafari and his friends advanced. "What do you want, Tafari?"

Tafari smirked, crossing his arms. "Is it true what they say? That you control the weather and can hurt people with your touch?" he taunted. "If you're so powerful, why don't you just make us all disappear?"

Almanza's heart pounded, anger flickering in her chest. She forced herself to stay calm, remembering her mother's words, but Tafari's mocking laughter grated on her nerves. "I only use my powers to help people, Tafari," she replied, her voice trembling slightly. "I would never harm anyone."

"Oh, really?" he scoffed, stepping closer. "That's not what people are saying. They say you're cursed, that your magic will bring ruin to Maputo. You might think you're special, but you're just a freak!"

Almanza's face flushed, and she clenched her fists, feeling a surge of heat building within her. Just as the first raindrops began to fall from the sky, Nia and Kofi arrived, rushing to her side. They had been looking for her and had overheard part of the exchange.

Kofi, always quick to defend his friends, stepped forward, glaring at Tafari. "Leave her alone, Tafari! Almanza has done nothing to you!"

Nia put a comforting hand on Almanza's shoulder, whispering, "Don't let him get to you, Almanza. You're better than him."

But Tafari sneered, undeterred. "Oh, look at her protectors. Do you really trust her? One wrong move, and who knows what she'll do."

Kofi shot him a sharp look. "You don't know anything, Tafari. Almanza's powers are a gift, and she uses them to help people."

Tafari laughed, a bitter, mocking sound. "Maybe now, but what about when she gets mad? I've heard stories—stories about lightning coming from her hands. Do you really think she can control herself?"

Almanza's breathing quickened as her anger simmered dangerously close to the surface. Memories of the last time she had felt this way—the uncontrollable storm that had raged for days—flashed in her mind. She tried to calm herself, focusing on Nia's soothing presence and Kofi's protective stance beside her.

Kofi stepped closer, blocking Tafari from getting nearer to Almanza. "She has more strength and kindness than you'll ever understand, Tafari," he said firmly. "Now leave, before I make you."

For a moment, Tafari faltered, his smug expression wavering as he glanced at Kofi's determined face and the hint of power flickering in Almanza's gaze. He hesitated, then scowled, muttering under his breath as he motioned for his friends to follow. "Whatever. Let's go," he grumbled, casting one last hateful glance at Almanza before turning away.

As Tafari and his followers left, Nia turned to Almanza, her eyes full of concern. "Are you okay? Don't listen to him. He's just jealous and scared of what he doesn't understand."

Kofi placed a reassuring hand on Almanza's shoulder. "You don't need to prove anything to anyone, Almanza. We know who you really are."

Almanza looked down, a tear slipping down her cheek. "I just don't understand. I only wanted to help, and now it feels like everything I do makes them afraid of me."

Nia gave her a gentle hug. "People fear what they don't know, Almanza. But Kofi and I aren't afraid. We know you, and we'll always be here for you."

Kofi nodded, his face serious. "Remember last time, when you were this upset?" he whispered, glancing up at the sky. "It rained for three days, and lightning even struck near the village. You have to stay calm, Almanza. We don't want that to happen again."

Almanza closed her eyes, taking a deep breath as she tried to steady her emotions. She focused on her friends' comforting presence, letting their support wash over her like a soothing balm. Gradually, the anger that had flared within her began to subside, and the tension in the air eased, the raindrops fading as quickly as they had come.

"Thank you," she whispered, looking at Nia and Kofi with gratitude. "I don't know what I'd do without you both."

Nia smiled warmly. "You don't have to face any of this alone. We're a team, remember?"

Kofi grinned, giving her a playful nudge. "And don't forget, you're royalty. We'll remind anyone who tries to mess with you."

Almanza laughed softly, the warmth of her friends lifting her spirits. Though the pain of the villagers' suspicion weighed heavily on her, she felt stronger knowing she had Nia and Kofi by her side.

That evening, Almanza told her mother what had happened. Adisa listened intently, her face a mixture of concern and pride. When Almanza finished, Adisa gently took her hands, her voice filled with both love and resolve.

"My daughter, there will always be those who fear what they do not understand. Your gifts are rare, and rare things often invite both admiration and jealousy. But never forget that your heart is what defines you. Use your powers wisely, with kindness, and in time, people will see your true nature."

Almanza looked up at her mother, her resolve strengthened by her words. "I'll try, Mama. I'll show them that my powers can bring good, no matter what they think."

Adisa smiled, pride shining in her eyes. "And I'll be here with you, every step of the way."

Together, they sat in silence, the weight of the day's events settling over them. Adisa knew that this was only the beginning of Almanza's journey, but she also knew that her daughter's strength and compassion would guide her through the trials ahead. And as the stars filled the sky over Maputo, Almanza felt a renewed sense of purpose, determined to prove that her powers could be a force for good, no matter the doubts of those around her.

CHAPTER NINE

An Unexpected Visitor

IN THE VILLAGE OF Maputo, life unfolded with a steady rhythm. But beneath the surface calm, whispers had begun to spread—rumors of Almanza's powers and the extraordinary gifts possessed by the young girl with the green eyes. Her acts of healing had reached ears far beyond Maputo's borders, and the story of her powers had stirred curiosity—and perhaps envy—in distant places.

It was early one morning, just as the first light painted the sky in soft hues of pink and gold, when a figure appeared on the horizon, casting a long, solitary shadow across the fields. Dressed in a dark, billowing cloak, the traveler moved purposefully, his silhouette merging with the early morning mist. His appearance was striking, his presence unsettling, a strange sight against the quiet backdrop of village life.

As the villagers went about their early tasks, news of the stranger's approach spread quickly. Soon, a small crowd gathered near the village square, their expressions ranging from curiosity to apprehension. Queen Adisa, informed by one of her guards, was alerted to the presence of this unexpected guest and resolved to meet him herself. Though cautious, she was also a gracious leader and believed in extending a welcome, even when caution lingered in the air.

Adisa approached the square with Almanza by her side. The queen's dignified presence parted the crowd, her calm authority soothing the murmur of questions and concern that had risen among the villagers. Almanza stayed close, her heart pounding with both intrigue and caution.

As they approached, the traveler lifted his hood, revealing a face both sharp and unreadable. His dark eyes held an intensity that seemed to pierce through the still morning air, making the villagers' whispers fade to silence.

"Greetings, traveler," Adisa began, her voice strong yet calm. "I am Queen Adisa of Maputo. May I ask the reason for your visit?"

The man inclined his head respectfully, his movements measured and graceful. "Your Majesty," he replied in a deep, steady voice, "my name is Malosi, a seeker of knowledge. I have traveled far and heard stories of a girl with green eyes who possesses rare gifts. I come to Maputo to meet this child and to offer my insights into the nature of her powers."

A ripple of uncertainty passed through the crowd, but Adisa held his gaze. "Almanza is my daughter, and her abilities are indeed remarkable. But she is young and still learning. What is it that you seek from her?"

Malosi's gaze softened, though his eyes remained intense. "I wish to understand her powers, to explore the mysteries within them. My journey has brought me to many lands, and I have encountered those who wield magic with wisdom and others who wield it with caution. I hope to offer guidance to those who seek it."

Almanza's curiosity was piqued. She studied the traveler, sensing both knowledge and something concealed, something he was not yet ready to reveal. Adisa, however, was vigilant, aware that not all who sought out magical abilities did so with pure intentions.

After a brief pause, Adisa nodded. "Very well, Malosi. You may speak with my daughter, but know that I am her protector, and her well-being is my utmost priority."

Malosi nodded, his expression a mixture of respect and subtle triumph. "I understand, Your Majesty. I assure you, my intentions are pure. My wish is only to help her refine her powers and to prepare her for the path that lies ahead."

Adisa signaled to her guards to escort Malosi to a private chamber within the palace, where he and Almanza could speak. The palace was adorned with rich fabrics and intricate carvings that reflected Maputo's beauty and strength, its walls imbued with the history and legacy of her ancestors.

Once inside, Malosi turned to Almanza, a soft smile breaking his stern demeanor. "Almanza, I have heard of your healing abilities. They are impressive for one so young. Tell me, how do you feel when you use your magic?"

Almanza hesitated, casting a quick glance at her mother before speaking. "I feel... connected. Like I'm part of something bigger than myself. But sometimes, it's overwhelming."

Malosi nodded approvingly, leaning forward slightly. "That is the essence of true magic—a bridge between yourself and the world around you. It takes discipline to channel that energy, to control it so that it flows as you intend. I have met others with similar gifts, and I believe I can help you refine yours."

Adisa, still vigilant, observed Malosi carefully, noting the way he spoke to her daughter with such directness. "Your words carry wisdom, Malosi, but be mindful of your guidance. Almanza's path is unique, and her powers are deeply connected to our land and her heritage."

Malosi met Adisa's gaze, his expression respectful yet challenging. "I am aware, Your Majesty. But I believe Almanza's gifts transcend borders. There is much she can learn from beyond Maputo. And with time, she may discover strengths even you have not foreseen."

A tense silence settled between them, and Adisa's protective instincts flared. "My daughter's powers are not a curiosity for others to experiment with. Her gifts are a blessing and a responsibility, and they will be nurtured under my guidance."

Malosi inclined his head slightly, acknowledging her words. "Of course, Queen Adisa. I meant no disrespect. My offer is simply to broaden her understanding, to teach her methods of focus and control."

Adisa's gaze did not waver, but she allowed herself a slight nod. "We will consider it. Almanza's journey is her own, and she must be given time to grow."

As the conversation drew to a close, Malosi turned to Almanza one last time, his voice filled with a hint of mystery. "Remember, young one, that true power lies not in what you do but in how you understand yourself. Magic is as much a journey within as it is an outward act. Embrace your gift with humility, and it will guide you."

With that, he rose to leave, the air of finality in his movements. As he departed, Adisa watched him with cautious eyes, aware that his presence had stirred questions she could not yet answer. She turned to Almanza, whose expression mirrored a mixture of awe and confusion.

"How do you feel, Almanza?" Adisa asked gently.

Almanza pondered for a moment, her green eyes thoughtful. "I feel... inspired, but I don't know if I trust him, Mama. He seems to know things, but it's as if he's hiding something."

Adisa smiled faintly, placing a reassuring hand on her daughter's shoulder. "Your instincts are wise, Almanza. Trust them. The world beyond Maputo holds many wonders, but also many dangers. Remember that your strength lies in knowing who you are, not in the approval of strangers."

As they watched Malosi disappear into the distance, the village of Maputo settled into a quiet unease, aware that this encounter had marked the beginning of something new. The mysterious visitor had left his mark, and the future seemed to shimmer with both promise and uncertainty.

The path ahead was far from clear, but with her mother's guidance, Almanza knew she was prepared to face it, step by step.

As Malosi rose from his seat to depart, his dark eyes lingered on Almanza, a faint smile playing on his lips, revealing just enough curiosity to leave her uneasy.

" Almanza," he said softly, his voice like a low hum that seemed to carry the weight of ages, "I sense in you a gift that even the oldest lands would envy. I wonder... have you ever thought about what more you could achieve?"

Almanza shifted, her gaze darting to her mother, who remained composed but watchful. "I... I just try to help," she replied, her voice quiet yet firm. "I don't know if I need more than that."

"Hmm," Malosi murmured, his eyes narrowing thoughtfully. "Helping is noble, yes, but it is only a beginning. Real power—true understanding—comes when you look beyond just helping. It comes when you know how to shape the world around you, to make it yours. Have you ever felt that pull, Almanza? The urge to control what you touch?"

A flicker of excitement mingled with fear danced in Almanza's gaze as she considered his words, but before she could answer, Adisa's voice cut through the silence.

"My daughter's heart is pure, Malosi," Adisa stated, her tone cool but resolute. "Her powers are not meant for domination. They are a blessing to our village and a source of healing."

Malosi's smile tightened, his eyes glinting with a challenge. "Ah, but even blessings can be harnessed in ways one might not expect, Your Majesty. Healing, after all, can also be a form of power. Used wisely, Almanza's gifts could make Maputo thrive beyond imagining."

Adisa's jaw set, her tone sharpening as she replied, "I think we both understand, Malosi, that power can easily corrupt. I will not have my daughter wield her gifts recklessly."

Malosi inclined his head with a graceful, if slightly mocking, bow. "Of course, Queen Adisa. Recklessness would be foolish. But perhaps it is not reckless to dream of what she could accomplish with proper guidance."

Almanza looked from her mother to Malosi, feeling the tension between them and sensing an invisible line in the air, as if a choice was being quietly offered to her. "I don't know if... I don't know if I need anything more," she said, hesitantly yet sincerely.

Malosi's gaze softened, but the glint of intrigue did not fade. "That is fair, Almanza. But remember this: magic will not stay dormant. It lives and grows within you, seeking purpose. It is your choice how to use it, but choose carefully, for it will shape you as much as you shape it."

Adisa's expression darkened as she took her daughter's hand, pulling her a step closer. "Thank you for your insights, Malosi," she said, a clear dismissal in her voice. "But know that we will always choose wisely—for ourselves, and for our people."

Malosi studied the queen with a gaze that was unreadable yet intense, his fingers tracing the edge of his staff. "Very well, Your Majesty. But I'll be close. My travels keep me on the move, but something tells me I'll be drawn back to Maputo. After all, one can learn much from watching magic grow."

As he turned to leave, his smile faded, and his eyes met Almanza's one last time. There was something in that look—an unspoken promise or perhaps a warning—and she felt a strange, unsettling thrill that lingered even after he had disappeared beyond the palace walls.

When Malosi was gone, Adisa turned to her daughter, her expression a blend of concern and warning. "Remember what I told you, Almanza. Not all who come to us in peace come with good intentions. Malosi may speak of power and growth, but there is something in him... something I do not trust."

Almanza nodded slowly, still processing the encounter. "I felt it too, Mama. Like he wanted something from me."

Adisa's face softened, but her voice was firm. "Yes, he did. And when someone wants what they should not have, they will go to great lengths to get it. I will teach you to protect your powers, Almanza. You will not be an easy prize to take."

Almanza held her mother's gaze, her heart steadier now. "I understand, Mama. I'll be careful. But I also want to know more—about myself, my powers. Maybe... maybe even about Malosi."

Adisa frowned, gripping her daughter's hands. "Knowledge is a good thing, but caution is a better friend. You have a lifetime to understand your powers. Do not be swayed by promises of greatness from those who have not earned your trust."

A long silence stretched between them, filled only by the faint rustle of the palace banners in the breeze. Finally, Adisa spoke, her tone gentler. "Almanza, I have seen the power in you, the light that can heal and inspire. That is more precious than any words Malosi could say. Trust in that light, and trust in those who love you."

Almanza felt a warmth spread through her heart, grounding her once more. "Thank you, Mama. I won't forget."

As the day wore on, Almanza and Adisa watched the village return to its rhythm, yet a quiet unease lingered in the air. Malosi's presence had stirred more than curiosity—it had awakened questions, both in Almanza and in those around her.

But with each passing moment, Adisa knew she would guide her daughter, guarding her from any who would threaten the balance they had built in Maputo. And even as she sensed that Malosi's influence would not end here, she held her daughter close, ready to face whatever future awaited them together.

CHAPTER TEN

The Dangerous Proposition

THE VILLAGE OF MAPUTO was still abuzz with the aftermath of Malosi's visit. His arrival and abrupt departure had stirred curiosity and apprehension among the villagers, but for Almanza, his presence had left a deeper mark. She had spent countless nights pondering his words, feeling a strange pull toward the mysteries he spoke of. She felt caught between her loyalty to her mother and the tantalizing glimpse of a world beyond Maputo—a world that Malosi seemed to promise.

One evening, just as twilight cast a purple glow across the sky, Malosi returned to Maputo, moving silently through the shadows. Almanza had been waiting, drawn to the edge of the palace garden by an unexplainable pull. She found him standing amidst a circle of flickering lanterns, his dark, intense eyes fixed on her, filled with both admiration and something darker—an intensity that made her shiver.

"Almanza," he greeted her softly, his voice smooth and persuasive, "I see you came. The pull within you must be strong."

Almanza nodded, curiosity warring with caution. "I don't understand why you're here, Malosi. What do you want from me?"

Malosi smiled, his gaze unwavering. "It is not about what I want, but what you want, Almanza. I am here only to help you see the power within you, to show you a path where your gifts are fully embraced. Have you never felt limited here, as if there's more you could do—more you could be?"

Almanza hesitated. "Sometimes. But my mother says that my powers are a gift meant for good, to help others."

"Ah, Queen Adisa," Malosi murmured, his tone shifting slightly. "A wise ruler, certainly, but she cannot see the extent of your potential. Helping others is noble, yes. But it is only a small part of what your magic could achieve. Power, real power, lies in embracing the depths of your gifts, in breaking free from limitations."

Almanza looked away, his words igniting a spark of excitement within her even as a voice in her mind warned her to be careful. "But what would that mean, to 'embrace the depths'? I've always used my powers to heal, to bring balance."

Malosi's expression softened, his voice lowering to a near whisper. "Healing, balance—those are admirable, but they are mere fragments of the potential within you. Imagine a power that shapes the world around you, that bends nature itself to your will. Do you not feel it, Almanza? The pull of destiny, the call to something far beyond these village walls?"

Almanza swallowed, her heart pounding. "Are you saying... that I could be more than what I am?"

Malosi leaned closer, his gaze intense. "Much more. But it requires courage. The courage to step into the unknown, to venture into realms that others fear. Your powers,

Almanza, are unique. But to harness them fully, you must be willing to journey beyond the light."

Almanza's breath caught, a mixture of fear and thrill filling her chest. "And what does that mean? The 'realms beyond light'? Are you talking about... dark magic?"

Malosi smiled, and for the first time, she saw a flash of something dangerous in his eyes. "Darkness, light—they are simply two sides of the same force. True mastery lies not in fearing one or the other but in understanding both. You could be more powerful than any healer, any ruler—if only you have the courage to step beyond the boundaries of what you know."

Almanza's fingers trembled as she thought of the possibilities, of a strength that went beyond anything she had imagined. But a familiar voice echoed in her mind: her mother's warning to use her powers with wisdom and caution, to trust in herself and her people.

"What about my mother?" she asked, her voice a whisper. "She says that power can consume you if you're not careful. That the magic we use should serve a purpose, not control us."

Malosi tilted his head, his gaze softening. "Your mother has lived a life in which caution has kept her safe, but she does not carry the magic that you do. She does not feel the depth of power that stirs within you, begging to be awakened. Can you say you have never wanted more than what this village offers? Do you not feel a spark of something... greater?"

Almanza met his gaze, her heart torn. "Sometimes... yes. But what would happen if I took that step? What would it mean for me—for my village?"

Malosi's smile grew, his voice dipping into a tone both alluring and dangerous. "It would mean freedom, Almanza. Freedom from doubt, from fear. You would become the master of your fate. No one would dare challenge you, no force would be too great to overcome. The world would be at your feet."

He pulled a small, glowing crystal from his cloak and held it out to her. "Take this, Almanza. This crystal can connect you to the deeper mysteries of magic. It will show you things hidden, powers unimaginable. All you must do is embrace it fully, and the path to greatness will open before you."

Almanza hesitated, her hand hovering over the crystal. She could feel its energy radiating through the air, pulsing with an almost magnetic force that seemed to call to her. "But... what if I lose myself?" she whispered, her voice filled with fear.

Malosi's gaze softened, but his words were firm. "One cannot discover their true self without taking risks. You will never know what lies within unless you are willing to step into the unknown. Trust me, Almanza. I am here to guide you, to help you harness your gift. But only if you are willing to take that leap."

Almanza's hand trembled as she reached out, but just before her fingers could brush the crystal, a memory flashed through her mind—her mother's face, her voice reminding her that true strength lay not in unchecked power, but in control, in responsibility.

"I... I don't know," she stammered, pulling her hand back. "This is a lot to take in. I need time to think."

Malosi's expression remained unreadable, his eyes narrowing slightly as he tucked the crystal back into his cloak. "Very well, take your time," he said, though a note of impatience slipped into his voice. "But remember, opportunities like this do not come often. The choice you make will shape your future, and it is not a choice that can be undone easily."

He leaned closer, his voice a low whisper. "Power waits for no one, Almanza. But it does not linger forever."

With that, he rose, his figure melting into the shadows as he disappeared into the night. Almanza stood alone in the garden, her heart racing, her thoughts a whirlwind of doubt, excitement, and fear. She knew that the choice before her was monumental, that it could change everything she had ever known.

As she looked up at the sky, the stars seemed to pulse with a quiet urgency, mirroring the turmoil within her. She felt the weight of destiny pressing down, the allure of power mingling with the warnings her mother had given. Could she resist the pull of Malosi's offer? Or would she find herself drawn to a path that promised greatness—at an unknown price?

The air was thick with tension, and in that moment, Almanza realized that her journey was only beginning.

The choices before her would demand all her courage, and she knew she would need to find strength not only in her powers but within herself.

She turned and made her way back to the palace, her mind troubled and her heart uncertain. The allure of the unknown tugged at her even as her mother's voice echoed in her thoughts. And as she stepped into the darkness of the palace, Almanza knew that the path ahead would test her in ways she had never imagined.

As Almanza walked back to the palace, Malosi's words played over in her mind like an enchanting melody she couldn't silence. The promise of power, of understanding the depths of her gifts, was as alluring as it was frightening. She could feel her heart racing with each step, torn between her love for her mother and her loyalty to Maputo, and the chance to become something beyond the boundaries of the village, something unimaginable.

The halls of the palace were quiet as she entered, her footsteps echoing faintly. She was so lost in thought that she didn't notice Queen Adisa waiting for her near the entrance to her room. When Adisa spoke, Almanza jumped slightly, startled from her thoughts.

" Almanza," Adisa's voice was soft, yet laced with worry. " Where have you been? It's late."

Almanza hesitated, glancing away, unsure of how much to reveal. "I... I went to the garden. I needed some time to think."

Adisa studied her face, her eyes filled with both concern and understanding. "You've been different lately. Ever since Malosi's visit, there's a distance in your eyes, a weight on your heart. Tell me what troubles you, my daughter."

Almanza looked down, feeling the tug-of-war within her intensify. She couldn't ignore her mother's concern, yet she was reluctant to share everything that Malosi had told her. She didn't want to worry her mother, and yet, a part of her longed for Adisa's guidance.

"There are... things he said, Mama. Things about my powers," she began, choosing her words carefully. "He said I could be something more, something... greater. He made it sound as if I was meant for more than just healing."

Adisa's face tightened, her protective instincts immediately on high alert. "Almanza, Malosi is a man of many words and hidden motives. Power can be seductive, but it is rarely as simple as it seems."

"But, Mama," Almanza said, her voice pleading, "what if he's right? What if there's a part of my magic I haven't yet touched? He spoke of understanding darkness and light, of not fearing what lies beyond. He said I could learn things that... that even you might not know."

Adisa's expression softened, her gaze filled with love. She reached out, placing her hands gently on Almanza's shoulders. "Almanza, your powers are a gift, but they are also a responsibility. Just because something is possible does not mean it is right. There are paths that lead to destruction, even when they appear paved with strength."

Almanza's heart twisted at her mother's words. "But how do I know, Mama? How do I know what's right or wrong with my powers? I feel something inside me, something that wants to grow."

Queen Adisa paused, her gaze intense. "You will know, my child, because you will choose with love, not with desire for power. True strength is not in magic alone but in wisdom, in kindness, and in the choices we make. Malosi speaks of a path filled with shadows, of power that might consume even the strongest heart."

Almanza closed her eyes, taking a steadying breath. "I just... I don't want to be limited. I don't want to wonder what could have been if I had dared to reach for more."

Adisa sighed, pulling her daughter into an embrace. "My dear Almanza, you have an entire life ahead of you. Patience will reveal what the heart is ready to know. Magic is like a river; it must flow naturally, at its own pace. Force it, and it might overflow, causing more harm than good."

Almanza felt the tension in her chest ease slightly, her mother's warmth and wisdom grounding her. "Thank you, Mama. I... I think I understand."

They stood in silence for a moment, the weight of the conversation settling over them. But even as Adisa comforted her, Almanza couldn't fully shake the whispers of Malosi's words. The promise of something unknown, something greater, lingered in her heart, a quiet echo that would not be silenced.

As Adisa stepped back, her eyes softened, filled with a love so profound that it reassured Almanza's troubled spirit.

"Go, my daughter. Rest. We will face this journey together, whatever comes."

Almanza nodded, but as she turned to leave, a part of her couldn't help but glance back, wondering if Malosi's shadow might return to haunt her once again. The mystery of his promise hung over her like a dark cloud, filling her with both dread and a flicker of anticipation.

That night, as Almanza lay in bed, the words of both her mother and Malosi swirled in her mind. The pull toward her mother's wisdom was undeniable, grounding her in love and purpose. But Malosi's words... they tugged at her, tantalizing her with visions of freedom, strength, and destiny.

She drifted off to sleep, her dreams filled with visions of a path shrouded in darkness and light, a path that promised both greatness and peril. Somewhere in the distance, she thought she heard Malosi's voice, soft and beckoning, calling her name.

The journey of self-discovery had only just begun, and Almanza knew that the choices before her would shape not only her life but the fate of Maputo itself.

As the night deepened, Almanza's dreams grew vivid and strange. She found herself standing in a dark forest, the towering trees casting long shadows under a crescent moon. A faint glow surrounded her, illuminating her path, yet everything beyond that small circle of light remained shrouded in mystery. She sensed eyes watching her from the shadows, and an unsettling thrill coursed through her as she walked forward.

Suddenly, the darkness parted, and there stood Malosi, his form bathed in a cold, silver light. His dark eyes held a magnetic pull, drawing her closer, and his expression was one of quiet intensity, as if he had been waiting for her all along.

" Almanza," he spoke softly, his voice like a whispered promise. " You've finally come. I knew you would feel the pull."

Almanza tried to respond, but her voice caught in her throat, the words lost in the silence. She took a step closer, entranced by the power that seemed to radiate from him, by the thrill of stepping into the unknown.

Malosi's smile was faint but dangerous. " You are at the threshold, Almanza," he said, extending a hand toward her. " Beyond this point, there is no turning back. But if you come with me, I will show you the path to true power, to a destiny that would make even the greatest rulers tremble in awe."

Almanza's heart pounded as she looked at his outstretched hand, feeling the pull of his offer, the magnetic force urging her to take that one final step. She knew that accepting his hand would mean stepping away from her mother's guidance, from the safety of Maputo, and from the path of light she had always known.

But the allure was almost overwhelming. Images flashed before her eyes—visions of power beyond her wildest dreams, of a world where her gifts knew no limits, of a life where no one would question or fear her abilities. She saw herself standing tall, her powers blazing like fire, commanding the elements and shaping the world around her. She saw freedom, strength, and an intoxicating sense of purpose.

Yet, amid the visions, she saw another face—the face of her mother, Adisa. Her mother's words echoed in her mind, grounding her amidst the storm of desire swirling within her. "True strength is not in magic alone but in wisdom... in the choices we make."

The visions began to fade, but Malosi's hand remained outstretched, his dark gaze locked onto hers, unyielding. "Choose, Almanza," he whispered, his tone growing more intense, more urgent. "Do you want a life confined by others' fears, or a destiny that is fully your own?"

With her heart pounding, Almanza's fingers twitched, aching to reach out to him. She opened her mouth, her breath shallow, on the verge of an answer.

Then, from somewhere far away, she heard the faint, familiar voice of Queen Adisa, calling her name. The sound was distant, yet strong, cutting through the haze of temptation like a sliver of light in the darkness.

"Almanza!" the voice repeated, sharper, more urgent, pulling her back from the edge.

Almanza blinked, her gaze shifting from Malosi's hand to his eyes. In that moment, she saw something she had missed before—a flicker of something cold, ruthless, lying beneath his smooth smile. The warmth of her mother's voice filled her heart, pushing back the lure of darkness, and she felt herself stepping back, her hand retreating.

Malosi's smile faded, his eyes narrowing as he realized her hesitation. His voice dropped, growing almost menacing. "Think carefully, Almanza. Refuse this now, and you may never find this power again. Choose wisely."

Almanza took another step back, her voice trembling but resolute. "I... I need time. This is not a choice I can make lightly."

Malosi's expression darkened, his gaze hardening as he watched her withdraw. For a moment, she thought she saw a flash of anger, of frustration, but he quickly masked it, his smile returning, colder than before.

"Very well," he said, his tone icy. "But remember, opportunities like this are rare. You cannot stay in the shadows forever, Almanza. You must either embrace your power fully or live forever limited, bound by others' fears."

With that, he stepped back, fading into the shadows as if he were never there, leaving Almanza alone under the cold moonlight. She felt a chill wash over her, realizing how close she had come to stepping into a world she didn't fully understand.

As dawn approached, she found herself back in her bed, her heart racing, her mind reeling with the gravity of her choice. She knew that her journey was far from over, and that Malosi would return, his words lingering like an unspoken challenge, a shadow that would follow her into the light.

And as the first light of morning touched the village, Almanza lay awake, torn between loyalty and longing, courage and fear. The path to her destiny was uncertain, but she knew that whatever choice she made, it would change her life—and the fate of Maputo—forever.

CHAPTER ELEVEN

Wrath of the Winds

THE DAWN BROKE WITH an eerie silence over Maputo, the air thick and stifling as if nature itself held its breath. But soon, the sky darkened, churning with ominous clouds that swirled into a fury overhead. The first crash of thunder shook the earth, and then the winds began—violent, unrelenting, ripping through the fields and tearing at the crops that the villagers had so carefully tended. Panicked cries echoed as people scrambled to secure their homes, clutching each other as lightning forked dangerously close to the rooftops.

In the heart of this chaos, Malosi emerged, his figure tall and imposing against the dark sky. His eyes blazed with fury, and his outstretched hands seemed to command the storm itself. Every bolt of lightning and gust of wind appeared to move at his will, intensifying the fear that rippled through Maputo.

Inside the palace, Almanza felt the storm's power like a pulse thrumming within her. She knew its source. Taking a deep breath, she summoned her own strength and hurried outside, where she found her closest friends, Nia and Kofi, standing amidst the chaos.

"Almanza!" Nia shouted over the howl of the wind, her face pale but determined. "What's happening? Why is Malosi doing this?"

"Because he's hungry for power," Almanza replied, clenching her fists. "And he's willing to destroy everything to get it."

Just then, a figure emerged from the shadows—the warrior Tafari, once the biggest enemy of Almanza but now one of Queen Adisa's most loyal protectors, his jaw set with fierce determination. "If we're going to stop him, we'll need every ounce of strength we have," he said, his voice steady. "I'll fight with you, Almanza. We stand together."

Almanza nodded, her resolve hardening as she looked at her friends and ally. "We have to face him, together. I don't know if I can control this storm alone, but maybe, with all of us…"

Kofi grinned, though his hands shook slightly. "Let's go show him what Maputo is made of."

The four of them moved as one, their feet pounding against the earth as they raced to the village center, where Malosi waited, surrounded by swirling winds and streaks of lightning. The villagers watched from the safety of their homes, faces pressed against windows, their eyes filled with both hope and terror.

When they reached him, Malosi's gaze fell on Almanza, a twisted smile stretching across his face. "So, the green-eyed child dares to challenge me," he sneered, his voice resonating with a dark thrill. "Do you think you can stand against the power of a storm, Almanza?"

"I won't let you harm Maputo!" Almanza shouted back, planting her feet firmly on the ground. "Your thirst for power has brought enough destruction. This ends here!"

Malosi laughed, a deep, mocking sound. "Then let's see what the chosen one of Maputo can do." He lifted his hands, and the winds intensified, whirling into a cyclone that threatened to engulf them.

Almanza closed her eyes, reaching deep within herself, calling forth the power she knew was waiting. Her hands began to glow, and the air around her warmed as she summoned the strength of the earth itself. Nia and Kofi stood beside her, their eyes fierce, while Tafari readied his spear, bracing himself for the confrontation.

Almanza opened her eyes, her voice steady. "Together."

Nia's voice rose above the storm as she called upon the calming energy she'd learned from the village healers, sending waves of peace into the air to push back against the rage of Malosi's storm. Kofi, always resourceful, used his agility to dodge lightning strikes, moving quickly to distract Malosi and weaken his control. Meanwhile, Tafari, with his warrior's skill, shielded Almanza and her friends, deflecting the harsh winds with every swing of his spear.

"Is that all you've got?" Malosi taunted, his hands crackling with energy as he shot a bolt of lightning toward Almanza.

She barely had time to react, raising her hands instinctively. The lightning hit her palms, but instead of burning, it melted into her, its power merging with her own. Almanza gasped, feeling the intensity of the energy flowing through her, and turned her gaze back to Malosi.

"You want power, Malosi?" she said, her voice laced with defiance. "Then here it is!"

With a fierce yell, she released the energy in a radiant wave, sending a shockwave that broke through the winds surrounding Malosi. He stumbled, momentarily thrown off balance, and Almanza saw her chance.

"Tafari! Now!" she shouted.

Tafari lunged forward, his spear aimed directly at Malosi, while Nia and Kofi surrounded him, their combined energy forming a protective circle around Almanza. But Malosi, though weakened, was not defeated. With a roar of fury, he retaliated, unleashing a gust of wind so powerful that it knocked them all back.

"Fools!" he spat, his face twisted in rage. "You cannot comprehend the power you face!"

Almanza struggled to her feet, her heart pounding. She felt the exhaustion seeping into her bones but forced herself to stand. She looked to her friends, who were battered but unbroken, each one wearing the same look of determination. They would not give up—not while Maputo was under threat.

"Almanza, we're with you!" Nia shouted, her voice steady despite the chaos. "We'll hold him back as long as we can."

Kofi grinned, his face streaked with dirt. "Let's give him a fight he'll never forget."

Almanza nodded, feeling their courage bolster her own. She took a deep breath, letting the warmth of the earth fill her. Slowly, she raised her arms, focusing every ounce of her power on calming the storm. She reached deep, finding the heart of her magic, and began to push against Malosi's energy, forcing the winds to still.

Malosi's face contorted with fury as he realized what she was doing. "No! You cannot take this from me!"

With one final surge of energy, Almanza poured her power into the storm, her hands glowing with a radiant light that spread outwards, blanketing the village. Slowly, the winds died down, the lightning ceased, and the storm clouds began to dissipate, revealing the clear sky once more.

Malosi staggered back, his face pale with shock and disbelief. "This... this is not possible," he whispered, his voice barely audible.

"It is possible," Almanza replied, her voice strong despite her exhaustion. "Because we protect each other. Because we stand together."

As the last of the storm faded, the villagers emerged from their homes, cheering and embracing one another, grateful for the calm that had returned to Maputo. Queen Adisa approached, her eyes filled with pride as she looked at her daughter and her loyal friends, each one a testament to the strength of their unity.

Malosi's gaze hardened, and he took a step back, disappearing into the shadows. "This isn't over, Almanza," he warned, his voice echoing through the quiet. "You may have won today, but the time will come when you will face your power alone. And when that time comes, you will be mine."

As his voice faded, Almanza's shoulders slumped, the weight of the battle settling over her. But when she looked around at the faces of her friends, her mother, and the villagers, she knew that she was not alone. She had people who believed in her, who would stand by her side no matter what.

Queen Adisa placed a hand on Almanza's shoulder, her voice filled with pride. "You've shown us all what true strength is, my daughter. Maputo will always be safe as long as you are here."

Almanza nodded, feeling a surge of warmth and purpose. She knew that her journey was far from over and that Malosi's shadow would continue to linger. But she was ready—ready to protect her village, her family, and everything she loved.

And as the village of Maputo returned to its peaceful rhythm, Almanza prepared herself for whatever challenges lay ahead, knowing that, together, they could face any storm.

As night fell over Maputo, a quiet settled across the village. The villagers, still shaken but safe, gathered around fires to share food, stories, and comfort. The threat of Malosi lingered in their minds, but for now, they celebrated their resilience and unity. Almanza, Nia, Kofi, and Tafari were seated near Queen Adisa, who had arranged a small gathering in their honor.

Almanza felt the weight of exhaustion pressing down on her. Her limbs ached, and her mind was weary, but a fierce sense of pride filled her heart. She had faced the storm, not alone, but with the support of those she loved and trusted most. She looked around at the faces of her friends, their eyes shining in the firelight, and felt a surge of gratitude.

Nia leaned over and nudged her. "I still can't believe we just did that," she whispered, her eyes wide with amazement. "I thought Malosi's storm was going to tear the whole village apart."

Kofi, sitting beside them, chuckled. "You're telling me! I thought that last gust of wind was going to send me flying into the river." He paused, his face growing serious. "But Almanza, the way you calmed the storm... it was like you were connected to something... bigger."

Almanza met his gaze, nodding slowly. "I felt it too. It was like I could feel the earth itself, guiding me. It wasn't just me—it was all of us, the whole village."

Queen Adisa's voice broke into their conversation. "Almanza, Nia, Kofi, Tafari—tonight, we honor you. Your bravery and strength saved Maputo. And your unity is a reminder to us all that we are strongest when we stand together."

Almanza looked at her mother, feeling the warmth of her pride and love. "Thank you, Mama," she replied, her voice soft. "But Malosi... he's not finished. He said he would return, and I know he's still out there, watching, waiting."

Adisa's face grew somber. "Yes, my child. Malosi is a formidable foe, and his hunger for power will not be easily sated. He is cunning, and he will try again. But tonight, we celebrate our victory and our resilience."

Tafari, who had been silent, cleared his throat. "Malosi is strong, but so are we. If he returns, we'll be ready. Together, we'll protect Maputo."

The villagers cheered in agreement, their voices lifting in unison, filled with renewed hope. For now, they had peace.

But even as they celebrated, Almanza couldn't shake the feeling that this was only the beginning of her battle with Malosi. His dark words echoed in her mind, a lingering shadow that threatened to disrupt the harmony they had fought so hard to restore.

As the night wore on, the firelight danced over the faces of the villagers, filling them with warmth and courage. Almanza looked up at the stars, feeling their distant glow as if they were watching over her. She knew that her journey was far from over, but she was ready for whatever challenges lay ahead. Her friends, her family, and her village stood by her side, and with them, she could face even the darkest of storms.

When the flames began to die down, Queen Adisa stood, signaling the end of the celebration. The villagers began to disperse, each one returning to their homes with renewed strength. Adisa placed a hand on Almanza's shoulder, guiding her back to the palace.

As they walked, Adisa spoke, her voice a gentle murmur. "Almanza, Malosi's power is vast, and he will not rest until he gets what he wants. But know this—you are not alone. You have a gift, one that will grow as you learn to harness it. And you have the love and support of Maputo behind you."

Almanza looked up at her mother, feeling the weight of responsibility mixed with hope. "I understand, Mama. I'll do whatever it takes to protect our village."

Adisa smiled, a soft, proud look in her eyes. "And you will, my daughter. Your courage and heart will be the light that guides us all."

They continued walking in silence, the quiet of the village a comforting presence around them. But deep within, Almanza felt a spark—a fire that had been kindled by the battle and by her connection to her people. She was ready to embrace her destiny, to face whatever lay ahead.

And as they stepped into the palace, Almanza knew that her path was clear: she would stand as Maputo's protector, ready to face any darkness that threatened her home.

The days that followed the storm brought a mixture of peace and preparation to Maputo. Almanza's battle with Malosi had shown the villagers just how vulnerable they were, and now there was an unspoken resolve in the air—a readiness to defend their home should the dark storms return. Almanza, Nia, Kofi, and Tafari spent their days training, each honing their own strengths, pushing their limits, and learning to fight as a unified force.

One morning, as the sun rose high over Maputo, Queen Adisa summoned Almanza to the sacred grove at the edge of the village. This grove, with its towering trees and ancient carvings, was a place where Maputo's leaders had sought guidance from the ancestors for generations. Today, Adisa and Almanza walked its quiet path side by side, the air thick with the wisdom of those who had come before them.

" Almanza," Adisa began, her voice calm but weighted with purpose, " I brought you here to teach you something every ruler must understand: power, true power, is not about control or dominance. It is about connection—to the people, to the land, and to oneself."

Almanza listened intently, absorbing her mother's words. " But Mama, Malosi's power... it was so overwhelming. It was like he was one with the storm itself."

Adisa nodded, her gaze distant. " Yes, Malosi's strength lies in his ability to bend nature to his will, but it's a power born from force, not balance. That is why he will never find true peace or fulfillment. His storm rages within him, and he lets it consume him. But you, Almanza... you must learn to control your power, to understand it so deeply that it becomes an extension of who you are."

As they continued deeper into the grove, Adisa gestured toward a large stone carved with the symbols of Maputo's ancestors. She placed a gentle hand on Almanza's shoulder, guiding her to kneel before it.

" Close your eyes, my child," Adisa said softly. " Feel the heartbeat of the land. Listen to the voices of those who came before us. They have always been with you, guiding you, protecting you."

Almanza closed her eyes, her breath slowing as she attuned herself to the energy around her. She felt the warmth of the earth beneath her, the rustling of leaves above, and the gentle hum of life that pulsed through the grove. A sense of peace washed over her, quieting her mind and steadying her heart.

As the moments passed, a faint glow began to emanate from the carvings, casting a soft light around them. Adisa's voice was barely a whisper, but it reached Almanza as if carried by the wind itself.

" Power tempered with love, strength balanced by wisdom... this is the path you must follow," Adisa murmured. " You are Maputo's protector, and the ancestors walk with you. Remember that you are never alone, even in your darkest hour."

Almanza opened her eyes, the weight of her mother's words settling within her like a steady flame. She nodded, feeling the strength of her ancestors flowing through her veins. " Thank you, Mama," she whispered, her voice filled with reverence. " I understand."

Just then, a rustling in the trees broke their moment of silence. Nia and Kofi emerged, their faces alight with urgency.

" Almanza! Queen Adisa!" Nia called, breathless. " Tafari's found something by the northern border. He says it looks like a warning... from Malosi."

Adisa's face hardened. " Show us."

The group quickly made their way to the edge of the village, where Tafari stood watch. He pointed to a series of dark symbols carved into the bark of a tree, twisted and sinister in appearance. The markings pulsed with an eerie glow, filling the air with a faint, unsettling hum.

" These are no ordinary marks," Tafari said, his voice grim. " It's a message... and a threat."

Almanza stepped closer, feeling a chill run down her spine as she examined the carvings. " What does it mean?"

Adisa's face was unreadable, her gaze fixed on the symbols. " It means Malosi is planning his return. He wants us to know that he will not be deterred."

" But why show us his intentions?" Kofi asked, his brow furrowed. " Wouldn't he have a better chance by attacking when we least expect it?"

Adisa turned to the group, her eyes filled with a quiet determination. " Malosi craves power, but he also craves fear. This message is meant to shake us, to sow doubt and anxiety among us. He underestimates the strength of Maputo and the unity of its people."

Almanza felt a surge of anger rise within her, her green eyes flashing. " Then we'll be ready. I won't let him harm our village. We'll prepare ourselves, strengthen our defenses, and if he dares to return, we'll show him that Maputo is not a place that falls easily."

The others nodded in agreement, their faces set with determination.

Adisa placed a hand on Almanza's shoulder, her gaze softening. " Remember, my child, the strength you draw upon is not only yours. It is shared with every person in this village. Let that be your guide."

Over the next few days, Almanza, Nia, Kofi, and Tafari worked tirelessly to prepare for the impending threat. The villagers banded together, setting up watch posts, fortifying their homes, and gathering resources. Adisa trained Almanza in the art of defense, teaching her techniques that combined both magic and physical strength. The elders gathered to bless the land, asking the ancestors to protect Maputo and grant them the resilience to withstand whatever might come.

One evening, as the sun dipped below the horizon, casting the sky in hues of amber and violet, Almanza found herself standing at the village's edge, gazing into the distance. Her heart felt both heavy and light, a mixture of fear and resolve settling within her. She knew the battle with Malosi would be unlike any she had faced before, but she also knew she was not the same girl she had once been.

As she stood there, Nia approached, her presence a comforting warmth beside her friend. " Are you ready?" she asked softly, her eyes filled with both worry and trust.

Almanza looked over at her, a small smile touching her lips. " With you by my side, I am."

The two friends stood in silence for a moment, watching as the last light faded from the sky. They knew that the coming days would test them in ways they couldn't yet imagine. But they also knew that, together, they could face whatever darkness came their way.

From the shadows, a figure moved silently—Tafari, his spear gleaming in the fading light. He joined them, his expression solemn. " If Malosi returns, he'll face a village that stands united. Maputo's strength is its people, and together, we're unstoppable."

As night fully embraced the village, Almanza, Nia, and Tafari returned to the heart of Maputo, where the villagers awaited them. Queen Adisa raised her hands, her voice carrying over the gathered crowd.

" Maputo has faced storms before, and we have always risen stronger. Malosi may return, but let him find us ready, steadfast, and unyielding. Together, we are a force greater than any magic, any darkness."

The villagers cheered, their voices rising as one, a sound that echoed through the night like a powerful incantation, filling the air with courage and hope. Almanza's heart swelled with pride and gratitude for her people. She knew that when Malosi returned, he would face not just her powers, but the unbreakable spirit of Maputo itself.

And as the stars blinked down upon them, Almanza felt the presence of her ancestors guiding her, preparing her for the battle that lay ahead. She knew the path forward would be difficult, but with her friends, her mother, and her people beside her, she was ready to defend her home against any force that dared to threaten it.

CHAPTER TWELVE

Ancestral Echoes

THE DESERT STRETCHED BEFORE Almanza in serene stillness, bathed in the soft silver glow of the full moon. After the storms and the whispers, the night air felt like a balm to her weary spirit. Exhausted and shaken, she needed guidance, and she had come to the sacred desert, hoping the silence would bring her clarity.

Almanza found a quiet spot on the smooth, cool sand, and settled down, crossing her legs and closing her eyes. She took a deep breath, letting the night sounds wrap around her—gentle rustling from the sparse shrubs, the distant call of a nocturnal bird, and the faint whisper of wind carrying secrets through the dunes.

170

" Why do I feel so torn inside?" she whispered to herself, her voice nearly swallowed by the vastness of the desert. " I thought I understood my purpose... but every day it feels like there's something more, something I don't yet see."

In her solitude, Almanza felt a flutter, and she opened her eyes to see Red Bird, her loyal feathered companion, perched on a nearby rock. Its fiery plumage looked vivid under the moonlight, a bright spot against the pale sands. Red Bird tilted its head, watching her, as if it understood the weight on her heart.

" You always seem to know when I need a friend, don't you?" Almanza smiled softly, reaching out a hand. Red Bird hopped closer, brushing its warm feathers against her fingertips in gentle reassurance.

Taking another deep breath, Almanza began to meditate, clearing her mind and focusing on the connection she sought—the guidance of her ancestors, the wisdom of those who had come before her. She called out to them silently, feeling a familiar warmth settle over her as she slipped into a trance, her mind sinking deeper into the sands of memory and time.

In the stillness, she felt herself transported. A golden light appeared, enveloping her, and one by one, figures began to emerge from the glow. Warriors with fierce eyes, rulers with dignified expressions, each adorned with symbols of strength and wisdom. They were her ancestors, bearing marks of power, their gazes filled with an eternal knowledge. Almanza felt their energy wrap around her, filling her with a sense of belonging.

One voice rose above the others, strong and yet gentle, like the soft rustling of leaves. " Almanza... child of our line, you carry the strength of many who have walked before you."

Almanza looked around, searching for the source of the voice, but all she saw were the shadowed faces of her ancestors. " Who are you?" she asked, her voice steady but filled with awe. " Why do I feel like I know you?"

Another voice, softer but filled with warmth, joined in. " We are your blood, Almanza. We have been with you since your first breath, guiding you, protecting you."

Almanza's heart ached with both recognition and longing. These voices—there was a familiarity in them that stirred something deep within her, like the comfort of a forgotten lullaby.

" I've felt you before, haven't I?" she murmured, her voice barely a whisper. " In my dreams... in those quiet moments when I feel strong."

A warrior stepped forward, his form flickering like a flame. His face was strong, his eyes fierce, and across his chest was a mark that looked like the symbol of Maputo, emblazoned with intricate patterns of strength. " Yes, child. We are with you in the moments you need us most, when courage rises in your heart. The path you walk is not new. We, too, have faced darkness."

Almanza's voice trembled as she spoke. " But why me? Why was I given these powers? I'm not of royal blood. I'm just... me."

The soft, guiding voice spoke again, filled with compassion. " You are part of a legacy, Almanza, one not bound by royal blood but by spirit. It is your heart that chose you, not your lineage. You were born to protect, to be a beacon for Maputo, as we were."

Almanza felt tears prick at her eyes as she listened, the weight of their words filling her with both pride and fear. " But it's so much, so overwhelming. How can I carry all of this? Sometimes, I feel like I'm not strong enough."

Red Bird chirped softly from beside her, as if urging her to listen closely to what would be said next.

Another figure, this time a wise, older woman adorned in the garb of a healer, stepped forward. Her eyes held both warmth and sadness, as though she knew the sacrifices that came with such a life. " Strength does not mean you must bear the weight alone, Almanza. Strength is knowing when to ask for help, when to lean on those who love you."

" It's not weakness to feel fear," the warrior added. " Courage is what drives us forward despite that fear. Remember, each step you take is not yours alone. We walk beside you, guiding you, lending you our strength."

Almanza nodded, feeling the warmth of their spirits settle into her own heart. She realized now that this was her true power—not just the magic within her, but the connection to her ancestors, to the legacy of protectors and warriors who had walked this path before her.

" I feel you all with me," she said, her voice steady, a newfound resolve settling within her. " And I promise... I will protect Maputo. I will honor this legacy you've given me."

As the figures began to fade, the gentle voice whispered one last message. " We are always here, Almanza. When you feel lost, remember to look within. You carry the spirit of Maputo in your heart, a light that can never be extinguished."

The vision dissolved, and Almanza slowly opened her eyes. The desert was quiet once more, the full moon casting a silvery glow over the sand. She felt a renewed sense of peace, the strength of her ancestors a steady flame within her.

Red Bird chirped again, breaking the silence. Almanza smiled, reaching out to touch its soft feathers. " Thank you, my friend. You always know when I need you."

As she rose to her feet, she took a deep breath, feeling the calmness of the desert settle into her bones. This place, these spirits—they would always be here, a reminder of where she came from, a promise of the strength she carried.

And with each step back toward Maputo, Almanza felt ready to face whatever lay ahead, knowing that she walked not only with her own strength, but with the courage of generations past.

As Almanza made her way back toward Maputo, a quiet resolve settled within her, each step a beat in the rhythm of a new song she carried from the desert. Her connection to the spirits of her ancestors had transformed her fear into a focused sense of purpose, and she now felt the weight of her responsibility with a comforting clarity. Red Bird flew above her, a constant companion, its brilliant feathers glinting under the moonlight.

Halfway back to the village, she paused on a small rise overlooking the land. She let her gaze wander over the distant glow of Maputo's huts, her heart swelling with love and a fierce protectiveness. Her journey was far from over, but she knew now that she could face whatever came her way. She had her ancestors, her friends, and the spirit of Maputo itself to guide her.

As she stood there, a faint whisper seemed to carry on the wind, an echo of the voices from her vision. " Remember, Almanza... courage is not the absence of fear but the presence of hope. And you, child, are the hope of Maputo."

Almanza's eyes filled with determination. She took a deep breath, whispering her own promise into the night. " I won't let you down. I'll protect Maputo, no matter what it takes."

As she resumed her journey, she heard footsteps behind her, breaking the stillness of the desert night. Turning, she found Nia and Kofi approaching, their faces filled with relief and curiosity.

" We thought we'd find you here," Nia said, her voice soft but firm. " You've been gone for hours. We were worried."

Almanza managed a small smile. " I needed some time to think. But I'm glad you're here. I could use some company on the walk back."

Kofi glanced at her, his eyes searching her face. " Did you find what you were looking for out here?"

Almanza nodded, a serene expression on her face. " I did. I spoke with the spirits of our ancestors. They... they reminded me of who I am and why I'm here. I feel ready now. Whatever comes next, I know I'm not alone."

Nia's eyes softened, and she reached out to squeeze Almanza's hand. " We'll always be here for you. You don't have to carry this on your own."

Kofi grinned, a mischievous spark lighting his eyes. " And besides, we couldn't let you have all the fun. If there are battles to fight and enemies to chase off, you can count on us to be right there beside you."

Almanza laughed, her heart lifting. " Thank you, both of you. I couldn't ask for better friends."

They walked back toward Maputo in a comfortable silence, the weight of the night's revelations settling peacefully over them. As they neared the village, the first hints of dawn began to touch the sky, casting a warm, hopeful glow over the desert landscape.

Just before they reached the gates, Kofi broke the silence, his tone uncharacteristically serious. " Almanza, this Malosi... he's dangerous, isn't he?"

Almanza nodded, her face thoughtful. " Yes, he is. But he's not invincible. His power comes from fear and control, not love or purpose. And that's his weakness."

Nia looked at her friend, admiration shining in her eyes. " You're right. And we have something he'll never understand. We fight for each other, not just for ourselves."

Almanza smiled, feeling the strength of their unity in every word. " Exactly. And together, we're stronger than he'll ever be."

As they entered the village, they could feel a shift in the air, a readiness and resolve that mirrored their own. Maputo had withstood the storm, and the villagers now looked to Almanza and her friends with a newfound respect and trust. Queen Adisa, standing by the village square, watched them approach, her gaze filled with pride.

" Welcome home, Almanza," she said, her voice warm with affection. " You carry the wisdom of the desert with you. I can see it in your eyes."

Almanza embraced her mother, feeling the strength of her family's legacy flow through her. " I'm ready, Mama. Whatever lies ahead, I'll face it with everything I have."

Adisa smiled, her eyes shining with both pride and a touch of sadness. " I know you will, my daughter. Maputo is blessed to have you."

They stood together, the rising sun casting its golden light over the village, illuminating the faces of those who gathered around them. In that moment, Almanza knew that she was exactly where she was meant to be, surrounded by love, courage, and the strength of generations.

For the first time in a long while, her heart was at peace.

CHAPTER THIRTEEN

The Weight of Power

THE MORNING AFTER THE storm dawned bright and quiet, a sharp contrast to the chaos that had swept through Maputo the day before. Almanza sat alone in the palace garden, watching the soft breeze play through the leaves, her heart heavy with an unfamiliar weight. Her body ached from the strain of her magic, and her mind felt clouded with doubt and fatigue. She had defended her village, yes, but at what cost?

She closed her eyes, remembering the raw energy she had wielded against Malosi. The power that had surged through her had felt overwhelming, almost uncontrollable. " If I hadn't stopped... if I'd let it consume me... what would I have become?" she whispered to herself, her voice barely audible.

A soft chirp drew her attention, and she looked up to see Red Bird perched on a nearby branch. Its warm gaze seemed to comfort her, yet even her loyal companion couldn't dispel the fear that lingered within her.

As she sat in silence, her mother's footsteps approached, the familiar, calming presence of Queen Adisa easing some of the tension in Almanza's chest. Adisa took a seat beside her, observing her daughter with a knowing gaze.

" I can see the storm hasn't fully left you," Adisa said softly, resting a gentle hand on Almanza's shoulder. " Your heart still battles with the power you unleashed."

Almanza nodded, her eyes cast downward. " I never realized just how... vast it was, Mama. The magic—it felt like it was pulling me in, like it wanted to take over. I'm afraid of what it could do if I ever lost control."

Adisa's eyes softened with understanding. " Power, true power, is as much a burden as it is a gift. You carry within you the strength of Maputo, but it's a strength that must be tempered with wisdom. You are wise to recognize its weight."

They sat in silence for a moment, the sounds of the village waking up around them. Almanza could hear the villagers moving about, repairing damaged huts, and tending to the fields. She knew they had seen her battle with Malosi, witnessed the full force of her abilities. And now, she sensed a distance in their gazes, a cautious reverence that held a touch of fear.

" I feel... different," she admitted, her voice quiet. " Like there's a wall between me and the others now. They respect me, but it's almost as if they're afraid of me too."

Adisa took a deep breath, her expression thoughtful. " That line between admiration and fear is a delicate one. People often fear what they don't understand. And magic, Almanza, is a mystery to many. They see your strength, but they may also wonder what would happen if that strength turned against them."

Almanza's heart sank at her mother's words, the truth of them resonating deep within her. " But I would never hurt them, Mama. I love them. I'd do anything to protect them."

Adisa placed a gentle hand on her daughter's cheek, her gaze warm and reassuring. " I know, my child. And in time, they will come to understand that too. But for now, remember that it is not just your strength that defines you—it is your compassion, your humility. Power does not set you above others, Almanza. It gives you the chance to serve them."

Almanza nodded, feeling the weight of her mother's words. " But how do I control something that feels so... limitless? I don't want to lose myself in it."

Adisa gave her a small, knowing smile. " It begins with humility. Remember that your gift is not yours alone. It's a connection to the world around you, to our ancestors, and to this land. As long as you stay grounded, you will not lose yourself. Do not let your power define you; let your spirit be the guide."

Almanza sighed, her gaze drifting to the village beyond the palace walls. " I understand, Mama. I just... I feel so different from everyone else. It's hard not to feel isolated."

Just then, footsteps approached, and Almanza looked up to see Nia and Kofi coming toward them, concern etched on their faces. " Almanza, we've been looking for you everywhere," Nia said, her voice filled with warmth and relief. " Are you all right?"

Almanza managed a small smile. " Yes, I just needed some time to think."

Kofi sat down beside her, his tone light but his gaze serious. " Well, you don't have to think alone. We're in this together, remember?" He nudged her playfully, adding a touch of levity. " You're not getting rid of us that easily."

Almanza laughed softly, her heart lifting at their words. " Thank you, both of you. It's just... everything feels so heavy. I want to protect Maputo, but sometimes I wonder if my power is too much for me to handle."

Nia reached out, placing a comforting hand on Almanza's arm. " Your power is a part of you, but it's not all of you. The girl we know is kind, strong, and true. You're not defined by your magic, Almanza. We see you for who you are."

Kofi nodded, his expression thoughtful. " And we trust you, even if the others are still unsure. Just give it time. People need to see that you're still the same Almanza who's been by their side all along."

Almanza's heart warmed at their words, the fear that had gripped her chest loosening its hold. " I don't know what I'd do without you both," she whispered, gratitude filling her voice.

Adisa looked on, her gaze filled with pride as she watched Almanza's friends rally around her. " True power is not measured by magic or strength, but by the love and loyalty of those who stand with you," she said softly. " Almanza, as long as you have your friends, your people, and your heart, you will never be alone."

Almanza nodded, a sense of calm settling over her. " Thank you, Mama. And thank you, Nia and Kofi. I know now that I can face this, whatever it may bring."

As they sat together in the quiet morning light, Almanza felt the weight of her power, but also the strength of her bonds. Her friends' unwavering loyalty and her mother's wisdom grounded her, reminding her that her true strength lay not only in her magic, but in the love and support of those who believed in her.

In that moment, she understood that her journey would be a balance between wielding her gifts and keeping her spirit anchored. She was Maputo's protector, but she was also simply Almanza—a girl with friends, family, and a heart filled with hope.

And with that understanding, she felt ready to face whatever lay ahead.

As the morning stretched into the quiet hours of the day, the warmth of the sun began to gently chase away the coolness that lingered in the air. Almanza sat there, surrounded by the quiet whispers of the world waking up. The hum of life in Maputo—a distant, constant rhythm of hope and renewal—was comforting, yet the weight of the conversation with her mother still pressed down on her heart.

Kofi and Nia's words were a balm, but there was still a lingering doubt in Almanza's mind, a whisper she couldn't quite shake. She had been chosen to protect her people, to wield a power that few could ever imagine, yet the fear of losing herself in that power remained. " What if I become something I can't control?" she thought again, her brow furrowing.

Nia, ever perceptive, seemed to sense the turn in Almanza's thoughts. She leaned closer, her hand still resting on Almanza's arm, offering silent support. After a moment, she spoke softly, her voice filled with gentle encouragement. " I know you're scared. But what you've done—what you can do—it's not just about your power. It's about your heart, your choices. Remember that."

Almanza looked at her friend, her eyes filled with uncertainty. " But my heart... sometimes, I wonder if it's enough to guide me. What if I make the wrong choice?"

Kofi, sensing the depth of the conversation, placed his hand on Almanza's other shoulder. " You've been making choices all along, Almanza. Not just with your power, but with who you are. And I know you'll keep making the right ones." He smiled at her with that familiar grin, his eyes gleaming with trust. " It's not about being perfect. It's about doing your best—and letting the people who care about you help guide you."

Almanza felt a warmth spread through her chest at their words, a flicker of hope breaking through the fog of her doubts. She had been so focused on the weight of her own burden, the power she couldn't quite control, that she had forgotten the strength she drew from the people around her. They were right. Power alone couldn't define her. " I've always been more than just my magic," she realized.

Her mother, who had been silently watching the exchange, gave a soft sigh and placed her hand on Almanza's head, gently ruffling her hair. " Your magic will grow, Almanza, but so will your wisdom. You are not alone in this journey. As long as you remember that, you will never lose yourself."

Almanza finally allowed herself to smile, the weight in her heart lifting ever so slightly. She had so much to learn, so much to still understand about her powers, but for the first time since the storm, she felt a renewed sense of purpose. " Thank you, Mama. And thank you, both of you," she said, looking at Nia and Kofi. " I think I've been too afraid of the wrong things."

Nia chuckled softly, shaking her head. " Fear has a way of blinding us to what's right in front of us. But you're

MS. LJ HALL, PHD

stronger than you think, Almanza. And you don't have to carry this burden alone."

As the four of them sat together, the conversation drifted into a more lighthearted tone, the tension slowly melting away. They talked about their plans for the day—how they would assist with the rebuilding efforts in the village and check on the injured—and even shared a few quiet jokes. The weight of the world outside felt a little less heavy, and Almanza realized just how precious these moments were.

But just as the laughter settled, a messenger appeared at the entrance of the garden, his breath quick and his face grim. Almanza's heart skipped a beat as he approached, sensing that something was amiss.

" Almanza," the messenger began, bowing low, " there is news from the eastern border. A group of raiders has been spotted near the village of Zakhara. They're headed this way."

A cold knot formed in Almanza's stomach, and she stood, her body stiffening at the mention of raiders. The tension that had briefly lifted returned with full force, and her heart raced as her mind quickly shifted into the mode of protector. " How many?" she asked, her voice steady but laced with urgency.

The messenger hesitated for a moment before responding. " We don't know the exact number, but the scouts estimate at least fifty."

Almanza exchanged a quick glance with her mother, Nia, and Kofi. " I need to go," she said, her decision instant. " We can't let them reach Zakhara. We have to protect the people."

Queen Adisa stood slowly, her gaze unwavering as she met her daughter's eyes. " Go, then. But remember, Almanza—your strength is not just in what you can destroy. It is in what you can save."

Almanza nodded, her resolve hardening as she turned to the others. " Let's go," she said. " We leave now."

The group quickly gathered their things and made their way toward the edge of the village, the sun now climbing higher in the sky. As they moved, Almanza's heart pulsed with determination. She would not fail her people. Not now, not ever.

But as she glanced back at the village of Maputo—at the place she had always called home—she couldn't help but feel the heavy weight of what lay ahead. Her power was growing, but so were the dangers she would face. " I'm ready," she whispered under her breath, the words more for herself than anyone else. " I have to be."

And with that, she led the way, her magic humming quietly beneath her skin, waiting for the moment when she would need it most.

The air grew heavy with tension as Almanza, Nia, Kofi, and the messenger made their way toward the eastern border. The sky above was a brilliant shade of blue, but the threat of the raiders loomed like a dark cloud, casting a shadow over their path.

Almanza's heart pounded as they walked, each step a reminder of the weight she carried. She could hear the whisper of her magic under her skin, like a restless river waiting for a storm to break. " What if I'm not enough?" she thought, clenching her fists as they neared the outskirts of Maputo. Her mother's words echoed in her mind—her strength was not just in what she could destroy, but in what she could save.

But could she save them all?

Kofi, sensing the shift in her mood, fell in step beside her. " You're not alone in this, Almanza," he said, his voice low but filled with conviction. " We're with you. Whatever happens, we face it together."

His words were a balm to her troubled thoughts, though the uncertainty still lingered. " I know," she replied, offering him a small smile. " But sometimes, it feels like I'm being asked to carry too much."

Nia, walking ahead, turned slightly to offer a reassuring glance. " You're strong because you've already faced the worst. And you came out stronger."

Almanza nodded, taking a deep breath as they reached the village outskirts. The dense woods stretched before them, the path winding and narrow. " Let's make sure we're ready for whatever comes," she said, her voice now firm with purpose.

They approached the edge of the forest where the scout had last reported seeing the raiders. The air was still, almost unnaturally so, and the sound of birds and insects that usually filled the air had vanished. A deep silence pressed down on the group, and Almanza's senses heightened. She could feel the crackle of tension in the air, as if the earth itself were holding its breath.

" Stay alert," Almanza whispered, her voice barely audible. She signaled for the others to spread out slightly, their movements fluid and coordinated, born of years of training together.

The forest around them grew darker as the trees thickened, casting long shadows over the path. The ground beneath their feet became softer, and the air grew cooler. It was a perfect hiding place for anyone wanting to remain undetected.

As they ventured deeper, Almanza's mind raced. She could sense the magic within her, the untapped power waiting to be unleashed. She had learned to harness her abilities, but only in small bursts—just enough to defend herself and those she loved. She hadn't yet faced a true battle of this magnitude. But now, she could feel the challenge before her, and with it, a growing sense of responsibility.

" I won't fail them," she whispered under her breath, clenching her fists tighter.

The first sign of the raiders came when they heard the faint sound of voices in the distance. They were low, guttural murmurs, the language unfamiliar but filled with malice. Almanza held up her hand, signaling for everyone to stop. She crouched low to the ground, using her heightened senses to get a clearer picture of what lay ahead.

" They're close," she murmured, her eyes narrowing.

Suddenly, a movement caught her eye—a figure darting between the trees, too quick to be fully seen. " We're being watched," she said softly, her voice laced with tension.

Nia nodded, her hand instinctively resting on the hilt of her blade. " Stay sharp. We don't know how many there are."

Almanza nodded, but she couldn't shake the feeling that they were being led into a trap. She could almost taste the danger in the air, thick and suffocating. " I'll take the lead," she said, stepping forward.

Kofi and Nia exchanged a brief glance before nodding in agreement. They trusted Almanza completely, even if they knew how much she carried on her shoulders.

The group continued forward, their movements now even more cautious. Every step brought them closer to the heart of the raiders' territory. The sounds grew louder, and the shadows of figures darting between trees grew more frequent. Almanza's pulse quickened as they reached the clearing ahead.

And then they saw them.

A dozen or more raiders stood in the open, their rough clothes tattered and their faces twisted with greed and malice. They had been waiting, it seemed, anticipating their arrival. Weapons were drawn—swords, knives, and crude spears all aimed at the approaching group.

Almanza's heart beat faster, the adrenaline surging through her veins. " There's no turning back now," she thought.

But she didn't hesitate. With a steady breath, she stepped forward, her voice clear and commanding. " This village is under our protection. Leave now, and you may yet walk away with your lives."

The raiders laughed, a harsh, grating sound that echoed through the clearing. Their leader, a towering man with a scar running down the left side of his face, stepped forward. " You think you can stop us, girl?" he sneered. " We've taken villages far bigger than yours. Your threats mean nothing to us."

Almanza's eyes flashed with cold determination. " I don't need to threaten you. I just need to protect what's mine."

She extended her hand, feeling the surge of magic flow through her, gathering at her fingertips. The air around her seemed to shimmer with power, the earth beneath her feet humming in response. She was ready.

The raiders were not cowed by her words, and their leader raised a hand, signaling for them to attack. The clearing erupted into chaos as the raiders surged forward, weapons raised. Almanza's magic flared to life, a brilliant light that illuminated the darkening forest, pushing back the shadows.

But as the battle began, she realized that the power she wielded was only part of the equation. The true test would be how she controlled it—how she could protect without destroying everything she loved.

As the first raider charged, Almanza steeled herself. This was only the beginning.

CHAPTER FOURTEEN

The Path to Shongwe

THE SUN HAD BARELY set when Queen Adisa called for Almanza. The sound of her voice, carrying both grace and gravity, echoed through the grand corridors. Almanza sensed a shift in the air, a sense of finality in her mother's summons, and made her way to the queen's private chambers, her steps slowing as she approached.

When she entered, Queen Adisa was seated by the window, gazing out at the twilight sky. Her poise was unmistakable, yet tonight there was a softness in her face, a quiet sorrow that Almanza hadn't seen before. She looked not only like a queen but like a mother carrying an ancient burden.

"Almanza," Queen Adisa greeted, her voice gentle yet laced with something more. "Come, sit with me."

Almanza crossed the room and sat before her mother, feeling the weight of unspoken words between them. She had so many questions—questions that had been gathering in her heart since childhood. Somehow, she knew tonight was the night they would be answered.

The queen turned to her, her fingers tracing the edge of a silver pendant around her neck. "There is a truth I have kept from you, one that I knew would one day need to be revealed," she began, her voice barely above a whisper.

Almanza's breath caught, her eyes widening as her mother continued.

"I lost my sons," Queen Adisa said, her gaze drifting as if she were seeing a memory. "The future of this kingdom slipped through my fingers. I felt... as though I were cursed, as though the ancestors had turned their backs on me. For years, there was an emptiness I could not escape."

Almanza reached out, placing her hand over her mother's. "Mother, I never knew..."

Queen Adisa's lips curved in a sad smile. "No mother would wish her child to know such pain. But that pain was a part of me, a part of this kingdom. Then, one day, the ancestors brought me to you."

Almanza's heart fluttered. She had always wondered about the day she was found, alone in the forest, her cries piercing the silence. But hearing it now, from her mother's lips, gave that story a weight she hadn't felt before.

"I found you, crying—a sound so pure, Almanza, it was as if the earth itself was mourning with you. I looked into your eyes, and I knew you were destined for greatness. I could feel it as surely as I felt my own heartbeat."

Almanza felt a lump form in her throat. "I... I never knew how much you sacrificed to take me in."

Queen Adisa's hand tightened over hers. "You were never a sacrifice, Almanza. You were my gift. The moment I held you, I knew that my heart, once broken, was healing. And then I saw the Red Bird."

Almanza's eyes widened. She had seen the bird herself countless times over the years, a creature that appeared at the edges of her life like a silent guardian.

"The Red Bird?" she echoed, almost in awe.

Queen Adisa nodded, her eyes glistening. "Yes. It watched over me as a child, and over my brother as well. It has been our family's protector, a messenger from the ancestors. When I saw it near you, I knew it was no accident. The ancestors had sent you to me, Almanza. You were always meant to be here."

Almanza took a shaky breath, her heart racing. "Then... you believe I have a destiny?"

Queen Adisa's gaze softened, and for a moment, she looked almost vulnerable. "More than that, my child. I believe you carry a part of our lineage, a piece of something ancient, something powerful. You were meant to be raised as royalty. But there is a part of you I cannot explain—a part that even I do not know."

Almanza's thoughts swirled, her mind caught between disbelief and a strange sense of recognition. "I have always felt... different. Like a piece of me was missing, like I belonged somewhere else."

The queen took a deep breath, and her voice grew solemn. "That is why you must go to Shongwe. It is time for you to find the pieces of yourself that were left behind."

Almanza's gaze dropped, a mixture of fear and longing filling her chest. She had always known that her life in Maputo was only part of her story, but the thought of leaving her mother, her home, and the friends who had become her family was almost unbearable.

"Mother... are you sure?" she whispered, looking up at Queen Adisa with tearful eyes.

The queen's voice softened. "Almanza, you are my daughter, and you will always have a place here in Maputo. But you are also a child of destiny, a child of the ancestors. And now, you must go and find the truth for yourself."

Queen Adisa reached into a small carved box on the table beside her and withdrew a beautiful amulet. Its surface was cool and smooth, intricately engraved with symbols of protection and strength. She pressed it into Almanza's hand.

"This amulet has been passed down through our family for generations," she said softly, her voice filled with emotion.

"It carries the protection of the queens before us. It will guide you when words fail."

Almanza looked down at the amulet, feeling its weight, the warmth of her mother's hand lingering on it. She knew this journey was hers alone to make, but her mother's love and the legacy of her ancestors would be with her every step of the way.

Almanza reached out, embracing her mother, her voice choked with emotion. "I could not have asked for a better mother. Thank you... for everything."

Queen Adisa held her tightly, pressing a kiss to her forehead. "You are stronger than you know, my daughter. The Red Bird will watch over you, and I will be with you in spirit, always."

With a final glance at the palace, Almanza turned and made her way to the stables. She had always known this day would come, but the reality of it felt surreal. Her heart was heavy, yet there was a new resolve within her—a determination to face whatever waited for her.

The Farewell to Maputo

As she rode through the gates of Maputo, Almanza cast a glance back at the walls and towers, the familiar landscape of her childhood. Her thoughts turned to Kofi and Nia, the friends who had been her constant companions, her family in all but blood. She had chosen not to say goodbye, for the weight of it would have been too much to bear.

In her mind, she pictured Kofi, his laughter filling the air as he teased her about her "royal airs." She could almost hear his voice, warning her to be careful on her journey. And Nia, her bright smile lighting up the room, her loyalty and friendship an anchor in Almanza's life. They had shared countless nights beneath the stars, speaking of their dreams, imagining a future filled with possibility. To leave them behind now felt like leaving a part of herself.

"I'll come back," she whispered to herself, the words both a promise and a hope. "One day, I'll return."

With a deep breath, she turned her gaze back to the road ahead. Her mother's words lingered in her mind: You are the child of destiny. The path to Shongwe was uncertain, but it was also the path to understanding herself, to uncovering the truth that had always eluded her.

The Red Bird appeared then, its scarlet wings a flash against the evening sky. It soared beside her, as if silently urging her forward. She felt a strange comfort in its presence, a sense that she was not alone, even on this solitary journey.

Her horse, Nahla, responded to her quiet determination, moving at a steady pace as they traveled away from the only home Almanza had ever known. The sun dipped lower, casting long shadows across the landscape, and Almanza tightened her grip on the amulet her mother had given her. The symbols etched into its surface were unfamiliar, yet they felt like a piece of her—a connection to the legacy she was just beginning to understand.

As they reached the edge of Maputo's lands, Almanza felt a final pang of sadness, a mixture of love and longing. But beneath it all, there was a new sense of purpose, a strength she hadn't known she possessed.

With the Red Bird soaring above and the road stretching out before her, Almanza rode on, determined to face whatever awaited her in Shongwe. She would discover the truth of her origins, the source of her magic, and perhaps, finally, she would understand who she truly was.

And so, with a heart full of questions and a spirit of quiet resolve, Almanza left Maputo, knowing that her journey had only just begun.

As the sun dipped below the horizon, Almanza rode deeper into the wilderness, her heart caught between excitement and fear. Each mile took her further from Maputo, from the familiarity of the palace walls and the warmth of her mother's embrace. Yet with each step Nahla took, she felt herself getting closer to a truth she had always sensed but never fully understood.

The Red Bird flew ahead, a crimson blur against the darkening sky. Almanza watched it glide gracefully, its presence filling her with a strange sense of purpose, as though the ancestors themselves were guiding her. The bird seemed to know the way, weaving between trees, occasionally glancing back at her with a watchful eye.

She spoke aloud, her voice soft in the evening air. "Will you always be with me, then?" she asked, half to herself, half to the bird. "Will you show me the way?"

The Red Bird gave no response, yet its path remained steady, as if answering her with its silent loyalty.

The sky turned to twilight, a deep indigo spattered with stars. Almanza began to feel the chill of night, and with it, a pang of loneliness. She had chosen to leave without saying goodbye to Kofi and Nia, but now, in the quiet, she felt the weight of that choice pressing down on her.

Her mind drifted back to a night not long ago, one of the many nights she had shared with them under the open sky. They'd gathered around a small fire, laughing and telling stories, Kofi teasing her about her "adventurous spirit" and Nia playfully insisting that one day, they'd all go on a grand journey together.

"I thought you wanted to stay in Maputo forever," Kofi had said, his voice full of mirth.

Almanza had laughed, waving his comment away. "Maybe I'll surprise you someday. Perhaps one day, I'll venture off and have my own adventure."

But as she'd said it, she hadn't imagined it would be this soon—or that she'd be going alone.

A soft rustling in the bushes pulled her from her memories, and her hand instinctively went to the amulet at her neck. She glanced around, her senses heightened, and her heart quickened. The forest was alive with the sounds of night creatures, but somehow it felt different now, as though the shadows were watching her with keen eyes.

She whispered a silent prayer to the ancestors for protection, clutching the amulet tightly. "Be with me," she murmured, hoping that her mother's gift held the power of all the queens before her, as Adisa had promised.

Just as she steadied herself, the Red Bird descended, landing on a low branch just ahead of her. Its bright eyes met hers, and in that moment, she felt a strange warmth fill her, a quiet reassurance that she was not alone.

"It's almost like you can read my thoughts," she said softly to the bird, her voice barely above a whisper. "If you're here to guide me, then please... show me the way."

The bird let out a low, melodic sound, almost like a song, before taking off again, guiding her down a winding path through the forest. Almanza felt a renewed sense of courage as she followed, her thoughts focused on the journey ahead.

A Mysterious Encounter

The night deepened, and a mist began to settle over the trees, softening the edges of the world around her. Almanza kept her eyes on the Red Bird, trusting its path. But as she rounded a bend, she saw a figure standing by the side of the road—a cloaked figure, tall and still, as though waiting.

Nahla halted, sensing her rider's hesitation. Almanza gripped the reins, her heart pounding, her gaze locked on the stranger. The figure raised a hand in greeting, their face obscured by the hood of a dark cloak.

"Almanza of Maputo," the figure called, their voice calm and measured.

Almanza's breath caught. She hadn't expected anyone to know her name so far from Maputo, especially not on such a remote path. She straightened her posture, her hand still resting on the amulet as she responded.

"Who are you?" she asked, her voice steady but wary.

The figure lowered their hood, revealing an elderly woman with eyes as sharp as the stars above them. Her face was lined with age, but her gaze held a wisdom that sent a shiver down Almanza's spine.

"I am called Nandira," the woman replied. "I have awaited your arrival. The ancestors have guided me to meet you on your journey."

Almanza blinked, trying to process the woman's words. "The ancestors?" she repeated, her voice tinged with both wonder and disbelief.

Nandira nodded. "The Red Bird has led you here, and it was by their will that I knew of your coming. You are the one destined for Shongwe, and there are things you must know before you reach its gates."

Almanza leaned forward, curiosity overcoming her caution. "Please, tell me. What is it that I need to know?"

Nandira stepped closer, her gaze intense. "The path to Shongwe is not an easy one. You will face many tests, not only of strength, but of heart and mind. The ancestors' gift is not a blessing freely given; it must be earned. And though the Red Bird watches over you, there will come a time when you must walk without its guidance."

Almanza felt a shiver pass through her. She had known that her journey would be difficult, but hearing Nandira's words brought a new weight to her task.

"How will I know when that time comes?" she asked quietly.

Nandira's eyes softened. "When it does, you will feel it in your spirit. Remember, child of Maputo, that the power you seek lies not only in the land of Shongwe, but within yourself. The truth you are searching for has always been a part of you."

Almanza's hand went to her chest, to the place where her heartbeat thudded steadily beneath her skin. She felt a surge of resolve, a strength she hadn't known was there.

"Thank you, Nandira," she said, her voice filled with gratitude. "I will remember your words."

The old woman gave a small smile, then reached into the folds of her cloak, pulling out a small bundle wrapped in cloth. She held it out to Almanza.

"Take this. It is a gift from those who came before you," she said. "It may serve you well in your time of need."

Almanza accepted the bundle, unwrapping it to reveal a small, intricately carved stone, glistening in the dim light. The stone felt cool in her hand, and she sensed a quiet energy emanating from it, as though it held a piece of ancient magic.

"This is a talisman of protection," Nandira explained. "It is not powerful, but it will shield you in moments of darkness. Use it wisely."

Almanza nodded, tucking the talisman into the small pouch at her side. "Thank you, Nandira. I am honored to carry this."

Nandira's gaze lingered on her, the faintest hint of sadness in her eyes. "Farewell, child of Maputo. May the ancestors watch over you. And remember—you are never truly alone."

With that, Nandira turned and disappeared into the mist, leaving Almanza alone on the path. She sat there in silence, absorbing the weight of what had just transpired.

As she continued on, her mind drifted to Nandira's words, the warning that her path would be one of trials and revelations. She felt a strange mixture of trepidation and excitement, her spirit both cautious and ready for what lay ahead.

The night deepened, the stars growing brighter as she traveled further, and the Red Bird resumed its flight just ahead, its steady presence reminding her of her purpose.

Almanza reached up, brushing her fingers over the amulet at her neck. She thought of her mother, her friends, and all those who had been part of her life in Maputo. Though she rode alone, she carried them with her, and that thought filled her with strength.

As she pressed onward toward Shongwe, Almanza knew that whatever trials awaited her, she would face them with courage. The path to understanding who she truly was lay ahead, and with each step, she drew closer to her destiny.

As Almanza rode on, she couldn't shake the lingering feeling from her encounter with Nandira. The old woman's words echoed in her mind: The truth you are searching for has always been a part of you. The weight of those words settled in her chest like a secret, leaving her both curious and uneasy.

The Red Bird continued its flight just ahead, occasionally glancing back as if to ensure she was following. Almanza watched it, feeling a renewed sense of companionship with the creature. It had been there at her darkest moments, always watching over her from afar. Now, it felt like it was leading her closer to her true self, one wingbeat at a time.

"Where are you leading me?" she murmured to the bird, her voice barely audible.

The bird gave no reply, but its path took her deeper into the forest, where the trees grew denser, their branches entwining like fingers above her head. Almanza felt the air grow colder, the shadows stretching longer across the ground as night fully embraced the land.

Just as she began to wonder if she should stop to rest, she heard footsteps behind her—soft, deliberate. Almanza's heart quickened, and she turned, one hand instinctively reaching for her amulet.

Out of the shadows stepped Nandira, her figure emerging almost as if she had materialized from the darkness itself. Almanza's pulse steadied, a mixture of relief and surprise filling her.

"Nandira," Almanza breathed, "you're here again."

The old woman gave a small smile, her eyes gleaming with something Almanza couldn't quite name—an ancient wisdom, perhaps, or the weight of years spent keeping secrets.

"Yes, child of Maputo," Nandira replied, her voice soft. "I wanted to speak with you once more before you journey further. There is much you need to understand."

Almanza nodded, her curiosity deepening. "Please," she said, urging Nandira to continue. "I have so many questions—about my past, about Shongwe... and about the Red Bird."

Nandira stepped closer, and Almanza noticed how the old woman's gaze softened as she looked at her. It was almost maternal, as though Nandira saw something in her that reminded her of someone else.

"The Red Bird has watched over your family for generations," Nandira began, her voice laced with reverence. "It is a guardian spirit, a messenger of the ancestors. They chose it to guide those of royal blood, those who carry the spirit of the ancient queens."

Almanza's eyes widened. "So... the bird truly is a part of me? Of my destiny?"

Nandira nodded. "Yes. But it is not a guardian that protects lightly. Its presence is a reminder of the trials you must face and the sacrifices you must be willing to make. The Red Bird will only remain with you so long as you are true to the path set by the ancestors."

Almanza felt a pang of anxiety, realizing the magnitude of what Nandira was saying. "And... what if I fail?" she asked, her voice barely a whisper.

The old woman's gaze grew serious. "There will be challenges, Almanza, moments when you feel lost or doubt your strength. But remember, your journey is not only for yourself. It is for Maputo, for the kingdom, and for those who will come after you."

Almanza swallowed hard, feeling the weight of her role settle onto her shoulders. "I will do my best," she said softly, her voice filled with determination.

Nandira's face softened, and she reached out, placing a hand gently on Almanza's shoulder. "The path to greatness is never easy, child. But you have the strength within you. You may not see it now, but you are more powerful than you realize."

The old woman's words stirred something within Almanza—a quiet strength, a resolve that had been buried under years of doubt. She felt the amulet at her neck grow warmer, as though responding to the courage she was beginning to feel.

Nandira took a step back, her gaze lingering on Almanza as if committing her face to memory. "Before I go, there is one more thing you must know."

Almanza's heart raced. "What is it?"

"Shongwe is not just a place," Nandira said, her voice lowering to an almost reverent whisper. "It is a realm of magic, a land where the spirits walk among the living. You will encounter forces there that few can comprehend, forces that will test your heart and your soul. And there may come a time when you must choose between the path of destiny and the path of the heart."

Almanza furrowed her brow, trying to grasp the full meaning of Nandira's words. "What... what does that mean? What choice will I have to make?"

Nandira shook her head, her expression unreadable. "Only time will tell, child. But know this: whatever choice you face, trust in yourself. The answer will come when you need it most."

Almanza nodded, though uncertainty still lingered in her heart. She wanted to ask more, to understand the full scope of what lay ahead, but a part of her sensed that some answers could only be discovered through experience.

The old woman gave her a final, lingering look before stepping back into the shadows. "Farewell, Almanza. May the ancestors watch over you. And remember—you carry their strength within you."

With that, Nandira vanished, fading into the darkness like a ghost, leaving Almanza alone once more.

The Journey Resumes

Almanza sat in silence, letting the encounter sink in. The warning about Shongwe—its magic, its spirits—filled her with a strange mixture of fear and anticipation. She had always sensed that her journey would lead her to something profound, but now the stakes felt higher, the mysteries even deeper.

The Red Bird flitted down from a nearby tree branch, letting out a soft call that seemed to draw her attention back to the path. Almanza took a steadying breath, her hand brushing over the amulet and the talisman Nandira had given her. She felt the quiet hum of power in each item, as though they held fragments of her ancestors' strength.

"You're right," she murmured to the bird, "it's time to move on."

With a renewed sense of purpose, Almanza urged Nahla forward, following the Red Bird's silent lead. The forest began to thin as they traveled, the canopy opening up to reveal patches of starlit sky. Almanza felt herself sinking into the rhythm of the journey, each hoofbeat echoing in the night, steady and certain.

A Moment of Reflection

As she rode, Almanza's thoughts drifted to Queen Adisa. She remembered her mother's face as they'd said goodbye, the love and pride in her eyes mingling with sadness. She thought of the words they hadn't spoken, the dreams her mother might have had for her, and the sacrifices she had made to raise a child who wasn't her own.

Almanza's voice softened, almost a whisper to herself. "Mother... I hope I make you proud."

She imagined her mother's response—a gentle smile, a quiet word of encouragement. The thought filled her with warmth, even as she rode further into the unknown.

The Red Bird swooped down, circling back toward her, its crimson wings almost glowing in the starlight. Almanza watched it with a sense of reverence. The bird was her guide, her protector, and in its silent companionship, she found a comfort that eased the loneliness of the road.

"Are you... are you one of them?" she asked the bird softly, her voice carrying a touch of awe. "Are you one of the ancestors?"

The bird made no sound, but it hovered for a moment, its gaze locked with hers, as though answering without words. In that stillness, Almanza felt a quiet connection, an understanding that went beyond language.

With a sigh, she continued onward, her mind filling with thoughts of Shongwe and the trials she would face. The journey felt daunting, yet there was a new strength within her—a strength she hadn't known she possessed.

And so, under the canopy of stars and the watchful gaze of the Red Bird, Almanza pressed forward, feeling the weight of destiny and the quiet promise of the future in every step.

The road to Shongwe stretched long and winding, but she knew now, more than ever, that she was ready to meet whatever awaited her.

CHAPTER FIFTEEN

Allies on the Path

ALMANZA SHIELDED HER EYES as she gazed across the vast desert, the sun casting a warm, amber glow over the sand dunes. The Red Bird, her loyal guide, circled above before swooping down and landing beside her, letting out a low, melodic chirp.

Almanza chuckled, reaching out a hand toward the bird. "Thank you, old friend. I can handle it from here. Go back to Maputo and bring Nia. Tell her... tell her I could use a familiar face."

The Red Bird cocked its head, as though listening, and after a moment, it took off, its wings catching the light as it flew back in the direction of Maputo. Watching it disappear into the distance, Almanza felt a mixture of hope and relief.

With the Red Bird gone, she was truly alone. She sighed, taking in the stillness around her. Though she was anxious about the journey ahead, something in the desert's quiet beauty put her at ease. She took a deep breath and started walking, her steps sinking softly into the sand.

As she made her way across the dunes, a movement up ahead caught her eye. Two figures were coming toward her, their outlines growing sharper as they neared. Almanza instinctively touched the amulet her mother had given her, but kept her posture relaxed, watching them approach.

The first figure, a tall, wiry man with a gentle smile and a satchel slung across his shoulder, greeted her with a friendly wave. "Greetings, traveler," he called out. "May the desert treat you kindly."

Almanza nodded cautiously. "And may it treat you kindly as well. Who are you?"

The man extended his hand. "My name is Kito. I am a healer, traveling through these lands in search of herbs and plants. And this is my friend, Moyo."

The second figure, a broad-shouldered man with a steady gaze, stepped forward and inclined his head. "A pleasure to meet you," he said, his voice calm but reserved. Almanza noticed the glint of a blade at his side, though he made no move to reach for it.

"Almanza," she replied, shaking Kito's hand. She looked between the two men, her curiosity piqued. "What brings you both here?"

Kito smiled, a spark of humor in his eyes. "Ah, the same thing that brings all travelers together—a need for new sights, new experiences... and perhaps a little adventure."

Moyo glanced at Kito, his expression more serious. "We have our own reasons for being here. But if we're heading in the same direction, perhaps we can share the path for a while."

Almanza considered this, sensing no immediate threat from them. "Very well. I could use the company."

The three of them set off together, walking at a steady pace as they moved deeper into the desert. After a time, Kito glanced over at Almanza, breaking the silence.

"So, Almanza, what takes you across these sands? You seem like a woman with a purpose."

Almanza hesitated, unsure how much to reveal. "I'm... seeking answers," she said carefully. "Answers about my past, about where I come from. There are things I need to know, things I can't discover in Maputo."

Kito's eyes lit with interest. "A search for knowledge, then? Admirable. I know the feeling well. I spent years traveling in search of new remedies and treatments, always wondering what I might find just over the next hill."

"Are you a scholar, then?" Almanza asked, noting his thoughtful expression.

"More of a wanderer, I'd say," Kito replied with a smile. "I've studied under many teachers, each with their own approach to healing. I carry a piece of each of them with me."

Almanza nodded, intrigued. "And what about you, Moyo? Are you a traveler as well?"

Moyo glanced at her, his expression guarded. "Something like that. I'm not much of a talker, though. Kito is usually the one who handles introductions."

Kito chuckled. "True enough. Moyo prefers to keep his secrets close, but don't let his silence fool you—he's got a heart as big as any I've met."

Almanza smiled, sensing that Moyo's reticence was not hostility but simply a quiet nature. "Well, it's good to have a strong and silent companion on the road," she said. "Sometimes, words aren't necessary."

They continued walking in comfortable silence, the vast desert stretching out before them. Almanza found herself relaxing in their presence, enjoying the sense of calm that settled over the group. It was a rare feeling, a quiet that allowed her to simply be without the weight of questions or burdens.

After a while, Kito began humming softly, a tune that blended with the whisper of the wind. Almanza found herself listening to the melody, feeling its soothing rhythm wash over her.

"That's a beautiful song," she said. "What is it?"

Kito's face softened. "It's a lullaby my mother used to sing to me. She was a healer too, you know. Sometimes I think she taught me more through her songs than her words."

Moyo gave him a sidelong glance. "I didn't know you were sentimental, Kito."

Kito laughed. "Only occasionally. And don't act so tough, Moyo. I've seen you get teary-eyed over less."

Moyo rolled his eyes, though Almanza caught the faintest hint of a smile tugging at the corners of his mouth. "That was once, and it was a long time ago," he replied, a bit too defensively.

The trio shared a laugh, and for a moment, Almanza felt as if she were back in Maputo, laughing with Kofi and Nia under the stars. The memory brought a pang of homesickness, but it was quickly replaced by a sense of gratitude for these new companions who had unexpectedly brightened her path.

As the sun began to set, casting shades of gold and pink across the desert, they came upon a small, sheltered spot where the sand formed a natural hollow, offering protection from the wind. Kito began gathering small pieces of dried brush, and soon they had a small fire crackling between them.

The flames danced, casting flickering shadows across their faces. Almanza felt herself relaxing further, the warmth of the fire and the companionship creating a sense of peace she hadn't expected to find in the desert.

Kito looked at her, his gaze thoughtful. "You know, Almanza, I've met many travelers on my journeys, but there's something different about you."

Almanza raised an eyebrow, intrigued. "Different how?"

Kito tilted his head, his eyes narrowing slightly as though he were trying to solve a puzzle. "I can't quite place it. A strength, perhaps, or a sense of... purpose. It's as if there's something guiding you, something beyond what any of us can see."

Almanza considered his words, glancing down at the amulet around her neck. She thought of the Red Bird, of her mother's parting words, and of the journey she'd embarked upon. "There may be," she said quietly. "I don't fully understand it myself yet, but I do feel... something."

Moyo watched her, his expression unreadable. "Purpose is a rare thing in these lands," he said. "Hold on to it. The desert is vast and empty, and it can make a person feel... lost."

Kito glanced at Moyo, a faint smile on his lips. "Listen to him, Almanza. He may not say much, but when he does, it's worth paying attention."

Almanza nodded, meeting Moyo's steady gaze. "Thank you. Both of you. I wasn't expecting to find allies out here."

Kito chuckled, throwing another twig onto the fire. "Ah, but isn't that the beauty of life? You never know who or what you'll find just beyond the next dune."

The conversation drifted into a comfortable silence, the crackle of the fire filling the air. Almanza felt her eyelids grow heavy, the journey and the day's events catching up with her. Just as she was about to close her eyes, a familiar cry broke through the quiet.

She looked up to see the Red Bird flying toward them, its wings casting shadows against the stars as it approached. Almanza's heart leapt at the sight, but her excitement doubled when she saw another figure in the distance, a figure she would recognize anywhere.

"Nia!" she called, standing up as her friend ran toward her, out of breath but smiling brightly.

"Almanza!" Nia cried, her voice filled with relief. "You didn't think you could leave without me, did you?"

Almanza laughed, rushing forward to embrace her friend. "I sent the Red Bird, but I wasn't sure if you'd come."

Nia pulled back, her face alight with determination. "Of course I'd come! You're my best friend. Besides, who else is going to keep you out of trouble?"

Kito and Moyo watched the reunion with amused smiles. Kito extended a hand to Nia. "Welcome, traveler. I'm Kito, and this is Moyo." Nia shook his hand, her eyes twink

The desert was quiet as the four friends gathered around the fire, the flames crackling softly in the evening air. Almanza sat with Nia beside her, feeling a surge of warmth and relief to have her friend by her side again. Kito and Moyo sat across from them, both of them watching the newcomers with curiosity and camaraderie.

"So," Kito said with a grin, looking from Nia to Almanza, "this is the friend you sent the Red Bird to fetch?"

Nia smiled, nudging Almanza playfully. "That's right. Almanza thinks she can do everything on her own, but someone has to keep her in line."

Almanza rolled her eyes, but her smile was warm. "Nia has been keeping me out of trouble for as long as I can remember. I suppose it's good to have her here."

Moyo, who had been quiet for most of the evening, leaned forward, his gaze fixed on Almanza. "So you have power over the Red Bird?" he asked, his tone curious but cautious.

Almanza hesitated, looking down at her hands. "Not exactly," she admitted. "The Red Bird has always been a part of my life. It's... hard to explain. I think it has a mind of its own, but it seems to appear whenever I need it most."

Kito studied her, his gaze thoughtful. "A mysterious guide. Fascinating. I've heard of such things, but never met anyone who had a guardian spirit."

Almanza shifted uncomfortably. She had always known that her connection to the Red Bird was unusual, but she rarely spoke of it. Now, with the eyes of her new friends on her, she felt a sudden urge to prove herself, to show them that she was worthy of their companionship and trust.

Nia, sensing her friend's discomfort, put a reassuring hand on her shoulder. "Almanza's always been special," she said, smiling. "I think she has powers she doesn't even understand yet."

Kito's eyes gleamed with interest. "Is that so?" he asked, his voice gentle. "Perhaps you've felt glimpses of these powers before?"

Almanza nodded slowly, her thoughts drifting back to the moments when she had felt something stir within her—a quiet but intense force, like a current of energy waiting just beneath the surface. But she didn't know how to control it, and whenever it appeared, it felt like trying to hold a river in her hands.

"I don't understand it," she said softly. "Sometimes... sometimes it feels like there's something inside me. A light, a kind of energy. But it's unpredictable, and it only appears when I'm under great pressure or—" She paused, choosing her words carefully, "—when I feel very strongly about something."

Kito leaned forward, his expression one of encouragement. "Power often lies dormant until the right moment. Perhaps the journey to Shongwe will help you find it. Sometimes, the answers we seek lie within us, waiting to be uncovered."

Moyo nodded, his gaze never leaving her. "Power is a burden as well as a gift. But it seems the ancestors chose you for a reason."

Almanza nodded, taking in their words. A quiet sense of courage bloomed within her, a resolve to finally embrace whatever was within her, even if it was strange or frightening. She closed her eyes, reaching inward, hoping to feel some glimmer of that energy she'd sensed before.

For a few seconds, she felt nothing but her own heartbeat, steady and calm. But then, a warmth spread from her chest, a gentle pulse that grew stronger with each breath.

She opened her eyes, and immediately, her friends gasped.

"Almanza..." Nia whispered, her eyes wide.

Almanza blinked, realizing that her vision was somehow sharper, as if the colors around her were more vivid. Her friends were watching her with expressions of awe, and she caught her reflection in Nia's wide eyes. Her own eyes were glowing—a soft, golden light emanating from within, bright enough to cast a faint glow on her face.

Kito let out a breath, his gaze transfixed. "By the ancestors... I've never seen anything like this."

Almanza felt both wonder and fear as the energy continued to pulse within her, radiating warmth that spread through her veins like fire. She could feel her senses sharpening, her awareness expanding to the world around her—the flicker of the fire, the subtle shift of the sand beneath her feet, the whisper of the wind as it moved across the desert.

Moyo, usually reserved, leaned forward, his expression serious. "This is... remarkable," he said, his voice low. "I have met warriors and sorcerers with power, but yours is different. It feels... pure."

Almanza took a deep, steadying breath, letting the warmth fade. The glow in her eyes dimmed, and she felt the energy retreat, slipping back into the depths of herself. She closed her eyes for a moment, grounding herself, and when she opened them again, her vision had returned to normal.

Nia placed a hand on her shoulder, her eyes still filled with awe. "I always knew you were special, Almanza. But... this is beyond anything I imagined."

Almanza's face softened, and she gave her friend a small, grateful smile. "Thank you, Nia. I don't fully understand it myself, but... it feels like a part of me, like something I'm meant to learn."

Kito's face was thoughtful as he studied her. "The desert is a place of tests and transformation. I think you were meant to come here, Almanza. Perhaps this journey will help you unlock the power that's been waiting within you."

Almanza nodded, her mind racing with questions. She had always known that her journey to Shongwe would reveal truths about herself, but this was more than she had expected. The glow, the sense of energy—she felt both exhilarated and apprehensive about the possibilities that lay ahead.

Moyo, sensing her thoughts, gave her a nod of quiet understanding. "You're not alone in this, Almanza. Whatever comes, you have allies here. Powers may change you, but friendship and loyalty keep you grounded."

Almanza met his gaze, appreciating the weight of his words. "Thank you, Moyo. And thank you all," she said, glancing around at her friends. "I don't know what awaits us, but... it feels right to be here with you."

The group fell into a comfortable silence, each lost in their own thoughts. The fire crackled softly, casting a warm light over their faces as the night deepened. Almanza felt a profound sense of calm wash over her, a calm that was rooted in the knowledge that she was surrounded by those she could trust.

As they sat beneath the vast expanse of stars, Nia leaned her head on Almanza's shoulder, her voice soft. "Whatever this power is, Almanza, I know it's meant for something good. I believe in you."

Almanza placed a hand over Nia's, her heart full of gratitude. "I'm glad you're here with me, Nia. I couldn't do this alone."

Kito began humming softly again, his voice blending with the desert wind. The melody was soothing, a lullaby that filled the air with a sense of peace. Almanza closed her eyes, letting the music wash over her, feeling the warmth of the fire, the weight of her friends' presence, and the steady beat of her own heart.

In that moment, she knew that whatever trials lay ahead, she could face them. With these allies by her side, and a newfound strength stirring within her, she felt ready to embrace the journey with open arms.

And as the desert stretched out before them, endless and serene, Almanza drifted into a calm, dreamless sleep, knowing that she was exactly where she needed to be.

Chapter Sixteen

The Trials of Fire and Sand

THE DESERT STRETCHED ENDLESSLY before them, a vast sea of golden sand that rippled like a living entity under the scorching midday sun. The journey had already worn them thin, each step a laborious effort in the blistering heat, the air heavy with the stench of sweat and dust. With every passing hour, the sun seemed to rise higher, fiercer, and the land beneath them grew hotter, as if the earth itself was trying to burn them alive.

Almanza, the older and wiser of the group, walked a few paces ahead of the others, his eyes constantly scanning the horizon for any sign of shade or shelter. The lines on his face were deeper now, carved not just by age, but by the harshness of the desert. Still, he carried himself with the quiet strength that had seen him through countless trials in his life. Despite his years, he remained the anchor of the group—steady, calm, and unfailingly resourceful.

" I've traveled through this land before," Almanza said quietly, glancing back at the others. " It has a way of breaking even the strongest of men. But it doesn't have to break us. We can endure it together."

His voice, though low, carried a weight that demanded respect. His words seemed to offer a reassurance, yet there was no denying the strain in his eyes. The sun had begun to dip toward the horizon, and the temperature was beginning to drop, but not quickly enough to bring them relief. The freezing nights were just as deadly as the blistering days.

Moyo, walking beside Almanza, gave him a half-smile. " I've been through my fair share of storms, but this desert... it's a different kind of test."

" Yes," Almanza replied, his gaze lingering on the swirling sands ahead. " This is the kind of test that shows you what you're really made of. It's not just your body that breaks here. It's your spirit, your will. We must hold on to each other, even when the winds try to take us away."

As they trudged on, the wind began to pick up, whipping sand across their faces. They pulled their scarves tighter around their heads, their eyes narrowing to slits to shield themselves from the sting. The sound of the wind was deafening, like the growl of some unseen beast, and for a moment, they were all engulfed in the silence of their own thoughts.

It was in the midst of this silence that the first sign of danger appeared—two figures emerging from the dust, their forms barely visible against the endless backdrop of sand. They were cloaked in rags, their eyes hidden beneath the hoods of their garments. Their movements were slow, deliberate, as if they were predators stalking their prey.

" Stay alert," Almanza murmured to the group, her voice steady but firm.

Moyo's hand instinctively went to the hilt of his blade, his body tensing in preparation. " Who are they?" he asked, his voice low.

" Nomads," Almanza replied, her eyes narrowing as she studied the figures. " Survivors of the desert. They'll not take kindly to strangers."

The figures came closer, and soon enough, they stopped just a few paces from the group. The taller of the two, a man with a weathered face and eyes that gleamed like shards of glass, stepped forward.

" You are trespassing," the man said, his voice rough, like gravel scraping against stone. " This is our land. Turn back or face the consequences."

Moyo stepped forward, his posture confident, though the heat made his skin feel tight and raw. " We mean no harm," he said, his voice calm but firm. " We are just passing through. We seek no conflict."

The nomad's eyes flicked to Moyo's blade, then back to his face. A thin smile curled at the corners of his lips, though there was no warmth in it. " You speak well, warrior. But words are cheap in the desert. What guarantee do we have that you are not spies or thieves?"

Almanza stepped in then, her presence undeniable. " We are not thieves," she said, her voice commanding but without aggression. " We are travelers, as weary as you are. We seek only to pass through and reach the edge of the desert. We have nothing to offer but our words."

The nomad studied Almanza for a long moment, as if weighing the truth of his words. Then, with a grunt, he stepped back and waved a hand dismissively. " You have your passage, but remember this—this desert does not forget. Should you return with ill intentions, the sands will be your grave."

Moyo nodded, his hand relaxing on the hilt of his sword. " We will not forget your kindness," he said, his voice steady. " Thank you."

With a final, scrutinizing glance, the nomad turned and vanished back into the swirling dust, his figure swallowed by the desert.

The group exhaled in unison, the tension slowly easing from their shoulders. Almanza gave Moyo a knowing glance.

" Well done," Almanza said. " You handled that with wisdom. Words can often win battles where weapons cannot."

Moyo gave a slight bow of his head. " It's a lesson learned from you, old man."

The group continued their journey, but now, with the encounter behind them, the desert seemed to hold a quieter, more ominous tone. The sun had nearly set, leaving the sky a deep orange, and the temperature dropped rapidly. The air felt sharp and brittle, the cold of the night pressing in. Their breath misted in the air as they walked, the chill gnawing at their bones.

As night fully descended, they made camp, huddling close together for warmth. Almanza began preparing a small fire, his hands moving with practiced ease. The crackling of the fire was the only sound that broke the heavy silence.

Moyo, sitting near the fire, looked around at his companions, his eyes reflecting the flickering flames. " I've never felt so alive and yet so close to death," he said quietly, more to himself than to anyone else.

Almanza glanced over at him, his gaze soft but understanding. " The desert tests everything, Moyo. Your body, your mind, your very soul. But it also gives something in return. Something that can't be found anywhere else."

" You mean the bond we share?" Moyo asked.

" Exactly," Almanza replied. " The desert strips you bare. It forces you to rely on others, to trust in their strengths. We're not just surviving it. We're becoming something stronger together."

Moyo nodded, the weight of Almanza's words settling in. The fire crackled between them, the warmth pushing back the cold. For the first time in days, Moyo felt a sense of peace.

And so, as the night pressed on, with the wind howling outside their small circle, each of them felt the truth of Almanza's words. The desert had tested them, broken them, and yet it had also forged a bond stronger than anything they had ever known. They were no longer just travelers through the desert. They were a unit—unbreakable, steadfast, and bound by the trials of fire and sand.

As they settled into their blankets, the sounds of the desert outside seemed to fade away, replaced by a quiet understanding. They had survived another day, and tomorrow would bring new challenges, but they would face them together.

The night grew deeper, and the stars above shimmered in a cold, clear sky. It was a sight that would have been beautiful in any other place, but here, in the vast emptiness of the desert, it only reminded them of how small they were against the great expanse of the world. The wind howled through the sand dunes like the wail of some ancient creature, and the cold crept into their bones.

Moyo lay awake, his mind racing despite the weariness pulling at him. The day's events had left an impression on him that he couldn't shake. The nomads had been a threat, yes, but the real danger lay not in their blades or words—it was the desert itself, and the struggle to hold onto one's humanity when everything around you seemed determined to strip it away. He thought of the people he had left behind—family, friends—and wondered if they ever felt the same sense of urgency, the same pressure to survive that the desert forced on him.

But in this moment, under the same sky that had witnessed countless souls who had come and gone,

Moyo found comfort in something new. The presence of his companions—the strength they shared, the silent promises in their actions—offered him a reassurance he hadn't realized he needed.

Across the fire, Almanza sat alone, her posture relaxed as she gazed into the flames. There was something profound in his stillness, something that spoke of a life lived in harmony with the land, no matter how harsh or unforgiving. Moyo admired the man's ability to find peace in the midst of chaos.

" You've been quiet tonight," Moyo said, his voice breaking the stillness. " Not like you."

Almanza's eyes shifted slightly, though she didn't look directly at Moyo. " The desert has a way of making you listen to your thoughts more closely," she said, his voice low, thoughtful. " When you're alone in it—truly alone—you start to hear everything you've been running from. Not just the wind or the sand, but the things inside yourself."

Moyo remained silent for a moment, turning Almanza's words over in his mind. " I can't say I'm enjoying the silence," he admitted, the heaviness of the desert weighing on his words. " It feels too... vast. Too empty."

Almanza nodded slowly. " The emptiness is something to fear, yes. But it's also something to learn from. It's a reminder that we're only here for a moment. A breath. A flicker of light in the dark."

Moyo shifted uncomfortably. " What if we're not strong enough to face it?"

" You are stronger than you think," Almanza said softly, finally meeting Moyo's eyes. " The strength isn't always in fighting, Moyo. Sometimes, it's in simply enduring. In taking one step after another, no matter how small. You'll find your strength in the moments you least expect."

There was a quiet pause, and Moyo looked away, his gaze fixed on the fire. The flames danced like fleeting memories, and for a moment, he felt something shift within him. Maybe it was the weight of the words spoken, or perhaps it was the realization that, despite everything, he had survived thus far. They had all survived. Together.

The desert night seemed to grow even colder, and Moyo pulled his cloak tighter around him, grateful for the warmth of the fire. He glanced over at the others. Nia lay wrapped in her blanket, her face peaceful in sleep, while Kato sat near the edge of the camp, keeping watch. Despite the hardships, despite the danger they had faced, there was a certain tranquility in the way they had come to rely on one another, each one playing their part in the collective struggle.

A soft voice broke through his thoughts.

" I can't sleep," Nia said, her eyes opening to meet Moyo's. " The wind is... unsettling."

Moyo smiled gently. " It's always unsettling the first time. But you get used to it. The desert is alive in its own way."

Nia sat up, wrapping her arms around her knees. " I've never been this far from home," she admitted. " I've never been this far from everything I've known."

" We all have our firsts," Moyo said, his voice quiet but steady. " You're not alone."

Almanza, who had been listening, finally spoke, his tone as calm as ever. " We all start somewhere, Nia. We all have our places of comfort, the things that give us peace.

But sometimes, peace is found in discomfort. In pushing beyond what we think we're capable of."

Nia nodded slowly, her gaze distant, as if she were reflecting on the truth in Almanza's words.

The conversation fell silent for a moment, each of them lost in their own thoughts. The fire crackled softly, its warmth a small reprieve from the chill of the desert night. But even as they sat together in the small circle of light, the vastness of the desert loomed around them, a reminder of how much farther they had to go.

Suddenly, the sound of footsteps in the sand brought them all to attention. Kato was standing, his posture alert, his eyes scanning the distance.

" What is it?" Almanza asked, his voice steady but concerned.

" There's movement," Kato said, his voice low. " Out there, in the dunes. I don't know what it is yet, but it's not one of us."

Moyo's hand went instinctively to his sword. The desert had a way of creating illusions in the dark, but Kato's sharp instincts had rarely failed them before.

Almanza rose slowly, her movements deliberate. " Stay close," Kato said, his voice commanding, but calm. " Whatever it is, we face it together."

They gathered quickly, their faces set, their minds focused. The desert, for all its cruelty and desolation, had taught them one crucial lesson: they were stronger together than apart.

The wind howled again, as though the desert itself was warning them, but in that moment, they were ready. Ready for whatever came next.

The wind whipped around them in ferocious gusts, swirling the fine sand into the air like a living thing, stinging their skin. It was hard to see beyond the edge of their firelight, but the presence of something—or someone—out there was undeniable. The desert had a way of keeping its secrets, but the silence that followed Kato's warning made it clear that something was not right.

Moyo stood beside Almanza, his eyes scanning the horizon, trying to make sense of the shifting shadows. "What do you think it is?" he asked, his voice barely audible over the howling wind.

Almanza didn't answer immediately, her attention focused on the horizon. Her eyes, keen and perceptive, missed little. "I don't know," she replied slowly, "but it's too organized to be a mirage. We need to stay alert."

Nia, who had been quietly watching the unfolding tension, felt the weight of the moment settle on her shoulders. Her heart pounded in her chest, and she instinctively reached for her dagger, though she had no idea if it would do any good against whatever might be out there. " Do you think it's another band of nomads?" she asked, her voice tense.

Almanza shook her head slightly. " Could be. But nomads usually travel in larger groups. This feels different." She glanced toward Kato, who had already begun to move, positioning himself in the shadows, blending with the desert night. "Stay here," Kato ordered, his voice calm but firm. "Let me go see what it is."

" No." Moyo's response was immediate, his eyes meeting Almanza's with a sharp intensity. " We stick together. I'm not letting you go out there alone."

Almanza considered Moyo's words, then gave a slight nod of agreement. "We'll move together then. But keep your wits about you."

They waited for a few tense moments, listening to the whisper of the wind and the unsettling sounds of the desert. The shadows seemed to move of their own accord, and every slight shift made the air feel thicker. Then, out of the haze, a figure appeared, silhouetted against the dunes—a lone rider on horseback.

Moyo's hand instinctively gripped his sword, but Almanza raised a hand to stop him. "Wait," she said softly, his eyes narrowing as he assessed the figure. "Let's see who it is."

The rider drew closer, the slow, steady rhythm of his horse's hooves almost drowned out by the wind. The rider wore a long, dark cloak, the edges fluttering in the wind, and his face was obscured by a scarf and hood. As he neared the campfire, the figure stopped, allowing the light to touch his face.

Moyo squinted, trying to make out the features of the stranger. The man was older, with a weathered, sun-scorched face that spoke of years spent battling the elements. His eyes, sharp and calculating, studied each of them in turn before settling on Almanza.

" You're not from here," the rider said, his voice deep and gravelly, as though the desert itself had carved it out of stone.

Almanza regarded the man with cautious curiosity. " We're passing through," she said simply. " We seek no trouble."

The rider paused for a moment, as though considering the words. Then he spoke again, this time with a more measured tone. " The desert does not suffer strangers lightly." He leaned forward slightly in his saddle, his gaze shifting toward Moyo and Nia. " But it seems the desert has taken a liking to you, if you've made it this far."

"We've had our share of difficulties," Almanza said, her voice steady but with a hint of respect for the man's words. "But we've managed."

The rider's lips twitched into something that could have been a smile, though it was difficult to tell under the harsh light. " Managed? It's not enough to manage the desert. It will break you, or it will change you." He seemed to study them each for a moment longer, then turned his attention back to Almanza. " I am Amiri. If you seek safe passage, you'll need more than luck. Follow me, and I'll show you a place where the sand doesn't swallow you whole."

Moyo exchanged a glance with Almanza. The offer seemed genuine, but the stranger's words felt heavy with unspoken meaning.

" We are grateful for the offer," Moyo said carefully, " but we must ask: why help us?"

Amiri's eyes flickered with something unreadable. " Because the desert gives as much as it takes. And sometimes, you come across something worth saving, even in the wasteland. The question is not why I help you, but why you are still standing. Few others make it as far as you have."

Almanza looked to his companions. There was a quiet understanding between them. The desert was not a place where they could afford to trust just anyone, but their options were few, and their strength was beginning to wear thin.

" Lead the way," Almanza said at last, his voice calm but resolute.

Amiri nodded and urged his horse forward. " Stay close," he said, " and keep your eyes sharp."

The small group packed up their camp quickly, each of them moving in practiced silence. As they began to follow Amiri, the desert seemed to shift around them, the wind carrying whispers from places unseen. The firelight flickered and then vanished as they ventured further into the night, the only sound now the rhythmic pounding of hooves on the sand.

The journey was slow, the sand sinking beneath their feet, but they moved with a purpose, knowing that the path ahead would not be easy. Every step they took seemed to pull them further from the world they knew, deeper into the heart of the desert.

Moyo walked beside Nia, the wind biting at their faces. " You think we'll make it through?" she asked, her voice uncertain.

Moyo glanced at her, offering a reassuring smile. " We have each other," he said. " And that's enough."

Nia nodded, the weight of the journey settling on her shoulders. She didn't know what lay ahead, but with each step, she found a little more strength. And in the silent promise of their shared bond, she knew they were not as alone as the desert made them feel.

As they moved forward, the stars above seemed to shine brighter, as if watching over them, guiding them toward something beyond the endless sand. Whatever lay ahead, they were ready—together.

CHAPTER SEVENTEEN

The Whispering River

THE STEADY SOUND OF rushing water greeted them long before they saw the river. Its murmur had a strange, almost hypnotic quality, as if the river itself was alive and whispering secrets only the brave could understand. The path they walked had led them through thick foliage, and now the air felt cooler, the scents of damp earth and wet stone mingling with the scent of the wind. It was a relief after the unrelenting heat of the desert, but there was something about this place that made Nia feel uneasy.

" Stay close," Almanza said, his voice unusually soft, yet firm. His eyes were narrowed, scanning the surroundings as though sensing something beyond the visible. " This is the Whispering River. The stories about it... they're not just rumors."

Moyo glanced at him, confusion in his eyes. " What do you mean? Isn't it just a river? A body of water we can cross?"

Almanza shook her head slightly, her expression distant as she stared at the flowing water. " There's more to it. The river is said to be cursed, and many travelers have disappeared here, never to be seen again."

Nia felt the hairs on the back of her neck rise at his words, but she couldn't help but feel drawn to the river, the way its surface shimmered in the twilight. The whispers, soft and faint, seemed to call to her in a language she couldn't understand.

"I've heard the tales," she said, her voice barely a whisper. "They say that those who are brave—or foolish—enough to cross are pulled under by unseen hands."

"That's the story," Almanza replied, his eyes never leaving the water. "But I believe it's not the river itself that's cursed, but the spirits that dwell within it. The ancient ones... they guard this place."

Kito, who had been walking beside them in silence, suddenly broke in, his voice filled with defiance. " Spirits? Tales of curses? I'm not afraid of some river, or whatever it is that haunts it. I'll cross if I want to."

Before anyone could protest, Kito stepped toward the water's edge, his feet sinking slightly into the soft mud as he looked out across the flowing river. The mist rising from the water seemed to swirl around him, almost like an invitation. " I've crossed worse," he muttered, and before anyone could stop him, he stepped into the water.

The moment his foot touched the surface, the atmosphere around them seemed to change. The soft whispers grew louder, swirling around them in a chorus of voices. The air grew colder, and the ground beneath their feet felt as though it was vibrating with some unseen power.

"Kito!" Moyo shouted, his voice filled with alarm.

But Kito didn't stop. He waded further into the water, a look of determination on his face, until the current suddenly picked up, tugging at his legs. " This isn't normal," Kito grunted, his footing faltering as the water pulled him deeper.

"Get out!" Almanza shouted, her calmness breaking as she moved quickly toward Kito, reaching out with one hand. But before she could reach him, the river surged, pulling him down with unnatural force.

" Kito!" Nia screamed, but it was too late. The water seemed to swallow him whole, the dark depths pulling him under.

Almanza stood motionless for a moment, the tension in the air thick as the last ripples from Kito's fall faded away. Then she closed her eyes, inhaling deeply as if centering herself. Her lips parted, and she began to speak in a language that none of them understood—words that seemed to vibrate with power, resonating with the very air around them.

"Moyo, Nia," she said calmly, though her eyes remained closed, "this is not a curse. It is a test."

"What do you mean, a test?" Moyo asked, his voice tight with worry. "Kito's gone! We can't just—"

"I can feel it," Almanza interrupted, her voice serene but firm. " The spirits within the river are watching us. We must approach with respect, not fear."

Nia watched in awe as Almanza extended her hand toward the river. The water seemed to calm as she spoke again, her voice becoming more melodic, more like a song than a command. The whispers faded, as if the very river had paused to listen.

Then, a soft ripple spread across the surface of the water. Almanza opened her eyes, now glowing faintly with an otherworldly light. " The spirits are not our enemies," she said quietly. " They are protectors. We must make an offering—an offering of peace."

Nia stepped forward, unsure, but trusting Almanza's words. She had seen Almanza work her magic before, but this was something different, something deeper. Almanza knelt by the water's edge, and with a careful, deliberate motion, she took a small bundle from her pack—bundles of herbs, dried flowers, and a small stone carved with symbols of protection. She placed the offering gently on the surface of the water, whispering words of gratitude and reverence.

For a moment, nothing happened. The river seemed still, the air heavy with anticipation. Then, the water shifted again, slowly, as if the spirits were considering her offering.

A soft light began to glow beneath the surface, and the water's current softened, becoming calm and gentle.

Nia gasped as she saw Kito's form emerge from the depths, his face pale but his eyes wide with realization. The river had released him, not out of mercy, but because they had shown respect.

He coughed, sputtering as he reached the shore, and the first thing he did was look up at Almanza. "I... I don't know what happened. It felt like... something was pulling me down."

"You were tested," Almanza replied calmly. "The spirits needed to see if we could prove ourselves worthy. You will not be harmed again, as long as we show respect."

Kito, still trembling, nodded, his pride and bravado crushed by the encounter. " I... I should have listened," he admitted, his voice a little softer now.

Almanza smiled gently. "Sometimes, we must all learn the hard way."

The group stood in silence for a moment, feeling the weight of the experience settle over them. The river, which had once felt ominous and hostile, now seemed peaceful, almost inviting.

"We can cross now," Almanza said quietly, "but we must remain humble. The spirits have allowed us to pass."

Moyo stepped forward, his expression a mixture of relief and awe. " What happens now?"

" Now," Almanza said, a calm smile on her lips, " we cross together, with the spirits' blessing."

One by one, they waded into the river, feeling the pull of the current but no longer fearful. The water seemed to part for them, as though the spirits were guiding their steps, ensuring their safe passage across.

As they reached the other side, Nia turned to look back at the river, feeling a deep sense of gratitude and understanding. The Whispering River was no longer a place of danger—it was a reminder of the power of respect, of listening to the spirits that shaped the land.

And as they continued on their journey, the whispers of the river seemed to follow them, not as a warning, but as a quiet blessing, guiding them on their path.

The air on the other side of the river was different—fresher, cleaner, and full of the scent of moss and wildflowers. The dense trees that had lined the riverbank began to thin out, revealing a wide, open plain stretching toward the horizon. The landscape before them felt like a breath of relief after the trials they had already faced. Yet, Nia knew better than to think that peace would come so easily.

As they walked in silence, the weight of their shared experience with the Whispering River settled over them like a quiet mist. No one spoke at first. Kito was still shaking off the shock, his usual cocky demeanor replaced with a thoughtful quiet. Moyo walked with a steady rhythm beside him, his eyes forward, though the calmness he exuded didn't completely mask the curiosity that seemed to shimmer in his gaze. Almanza, as always, remained a few steps ahead, her presence calm yet commanding.

Finally, Kito broke the silence. His voice was subdued, more reflective than usual.

" I don't know what I thought would happen," he muttered, his eyes scanning the horizon as if searching for something. " But I didn't expect... that. It was like the river was alive, like it wanted to pull me in. I could feel it."

Almanza glanced back at him, her face unreadable. " The river is alive in a way, Kito. Not in the sense that you or I are alive, but in a way that ties it to everything around it—the earth, the sky, the spirits. They protect it, just as they protect those who approach it with reverence."

"I was too stubborn," Kito admitted, the usual bravado gone from his voice. "I thought I could take on anything... But it wasn't the river I was fighting, was it?"

"No," Almanza said softly, stopping in her tracks to turn fully toward him. "The greatest battles are often the ones we fight within ourselves. You tried to fight a force greater than you could understand. You learned the lesson you needed to learn, Kito. The river, the spirits—they don't ask for fear. They ask for respect."

Kito nodded slowly, though his thoughts seemed distant. Nia could see the change in him, a shift that hadn't been there before. He seemed to understand, at least for now, the depth of what they'd encountered. It wasn't just survival anymore; it was about humility, about seeing things beyond the surface.

"I think I understand," Kito said, his voice quiet. " I thought it was about strength. But maybe... maybe it's more about knowing when to surrender."

"Exactly," Almanza replied, her voice soft but firm. "The strength to surrender is often the truest kind of strength."

The others nodded, each contemplating the lesson they had just witnessed. It was a quiet understanding, one that bound them together even more tightly than before. It was a lesson that would remain with them, a reminder that they were not invincible, that there was power in respect, and even in submission.

As the sun dipped lower in the sky, casting a soft golden glow over the plains, they found a spot to set up camp. The world around them seemed to pause, as though giving them time to process the events of the day. The fire crackled softly as they settled down, each of them finding their place, still wrapped in the calm that had followed the river's trials.

Almanza, ever watchful, sat cross-legged by the fire, her eyes reflecting the flames as she meditated in silence. Moyo busied himself with preparing a simple meal, while Kito sat slightly apart, lost in thought. Nia, however, found herself gazing up at the stars, her heart full of questions and quiet wonder. The sky felt endless, a vast sea of lights above them, and for the first time since the beginning of their journey, she felt a sense of peace. The weight of the world didn't seem so heavy here, beneath this canopy of stars.

Moyo broke the silence once more, his voice calm but filled with curiosity. " Almanza, do you think we'll ever understand everything? All the things we've encountered on this journey? The spirits, the trials... do they all have a purpose?"

Almanza didn't answer right away, her fingers moving rhythmically as if she were tuning into something beyond the present. When she finally spoke, her words were thoughtful, measured.

" Perhaps we don't need to understand everything right now, Moyo. Sometimes the answers will come when we're ready for them. The journey we're on is more than the destination. It's about the growth we undergo, the lessons we learn along the way. Trust in that, and the rest will fall into place."

Kito, who had been listening intently, nodded slowly. " You're right. I've spent so much time thinking I need to control everything. But... maybe that's what the spirits were showing me today. Maybe it's not about control. It's about learning to trust."

Almanza smiled, a gentle, knowing smile. " Exactly, Kito. You're learning. And that's what matters most."

The night passed in a quiet, serene calm. There were no more whispers from the river, no more trials to face. Only the soft crackling of the fire and the steady, rhythmic breathing of the group as they settled in for the night. The stars above seemed to watch over them, an eternal reminder that they were part of something much greater than themselves.

The next morning, the sun rose slowly over the plains, painting the sky in shades of pink and gold. The journey ahead would no doubt hold new challenges, but for now, the calm they had found was enough. It was a brief, but precious moment of peace, one they would carry with them into whatever lay ahead.

Together, they moved forward—changed, humbled, and united by the lessons they had learned. The Whispering River had not claimed them, but instead, it had given them something far more valuable: the understanding that some forces were not meant to be fought, but respected.

CHAPTER EIGHTEEN

Shadows of Shongwe

THE JOURNEY TO SHONGWE had been long, each step carrying with it a weight that seemed to press down upon Almanza's heart. She could feel the village before she saw it, as if the very air around her held secrets, whispered just out of reach. The land seemed alive, breathing, watching them as they made their way through the dense foliage that led to the village gates.

When they finally arrived, the village stood before them, a cluster of thatched huts and ancient trees, woven together in a delicate dance of nature and tradition. The earth was rich with history, but there was an undercurrent of tension that hung in the air, palpable and unnerving.

The villagers gathered in the square, their eyes following Almanza closely as she stepped forward. They whispered amongst themselves, their murmurs like the rustling of leaves, soft and fleeting, but undeniably present.

Almanza could feel their gaze on her, a mixture of awe and fear, like they knew her before they'd ever seen her. She kept her head held high, her expression calm, but her mind was racing.

"What is it about me that makes them look at me like that?" Almanza murmured to Moyo, her voice barely above a whisper.

Moyo stood by her side, his face unreadable, though his hand rested on the hilt of his blade, ready for whatever might come. "You're not like them. You're different. They can sense it."

Nia, walking beside them, turned her head to look at the villagers, noting their curious stares. "It's not just your eyes, Almanza. They can feel something from you—something beyond what they know."

Almanza nodded, her green eyes scanning the faces around her. "I know," she said softly, her voice steady but laced with uncertainty. "I've always known there was something more. Something I need to find."

As they moved deeper into the village, an older woman stepped forward, her face weathered with age but her eyes sharp, like a hawk's. Her presence was commanding, even without words.

" You have the eyes of the one who walked before you," the elder spoke, her voice carrying through the air with authority. The others in the village grew silent, the whispers dying down as she continued. " The child born under the night of the great storm, the one whose blood carries the weight of secrets better left unspoken."

Almanza's heart skipped a beat, a cold shiver running down her spine. "My mother..." she began, but the words caught in her throat.

The elder's gaze softened for just a moment, but her words were firm. " Your mother left us with a promise, child. But that promise came at a cost. And your presence here, in this village, may open doors best left shut." She paused, as though considering Almanza's next words carefully. " Do not seek answers that will change the course of your path.

For some truths are more dangerous than the shadows that guard them."

Almanza took a deep breath, steadying herself. She had heard enough. The shadows of her past were closing in, but she was not one to turn away from the unknown.

"I have to know the truth," she said, her voice unwavering, despite the weight of the elder's warning. "I need to understand why I'm here, why I'm different. What happened to my mother? What am I meant to do?"

The elder's expression remained stoic. "You are meant to do what the village fears, child. You are meant to face the darkness that lies within this land." She stepped closer, lowering her voice so only Almanza could hear. "But know this: the answers you seek come with a price. You may lose more than you are willing to give."

Almanza felt the heaviness of the elder's words settle over her like a cloak. She turned to Moyo and Nia, who stood by her side, their eyes filled with concern, but also with unwavering support.

"I'm not afraid," Almanza said quietly, though her words carried the weight of a decision she knew would shape everything that followed. "I'll face whatever comes. I owe it to myself—and to my mother—to uncover the truth."

The elder's gaze softened, a faint flicker of something unspoken passing between them. "Then go. But remember, child—some truths are not meant to be known, and once uncovered, they cannot be undone."

As Almanza stepped forward, Moyo placed a hand on her shoulder, his voice calm but firm. "We're with you, always."

Nia nodded in agreement, her smile small but reassuring. " Together."

Almanza smiled back, the strength of her friends grounding her as she made her way toward the heart of the village. Her mind raced with questions, with fears she wasn't ready to face, but she knew one thing for certain: she would not turn back now.

The path ahead was shrouded in mystery, the shadows of the past drawing nearer. But with each step she took, she felt a sense of calm settle over her, as though the village itself was guiding her forward, despite the warning.

As they reached the center of the village, where the elders gathered beneath an ancient tree, the air grew still, as though holding its breath. Almanza stood before them, ready to learn what had been hidden from her for so long.

The eldest of the elders, an ancient man with deep lines carved into his face, spoke, his voice a low, rumbling whisper that echoed in the silence.

"We have waited for this day, child. The time has come for you to know what was lost, what was hidden. But remember, the truth may change you, and once you walk the path, there is no turning back."

Almanza nodded, her heart steady despite the weight of his words. " I am ready."

The elder's eyes searched hers, seeing something deeper than she could understand. With a slow nod, he gestured for her to approach the sacred fire that burned in the center of the village.

"Come," he said, his voice both a command and an invitation. "The truth lies within the flames."

As Almanza stepped forward, the flames seemed to dance higher, as if recognizing her. The air hummed with energy, and in that moment, she knew that this was the beginning of everything.

The village had not only seen her. It had known her long before she had arrived.

And now, the shadows of her past were waiting to reveal themselves.

Almanza stepped forward, the heat of the fire intensifying with each movement. The villagers stood in hushed silence, their eyes fixed on her, and the shadows seemed to stretch and twist in the flickering light of the flames. As she approached the fire, her heart pounded in her chest, her every step an echo in the stillness of the village.

The eldest elder, his voice a low murmur, spoke once more, his words filled with the weight of centuries. " In the flames, child, you will find your truth. But be cautious. What you seek may not be what you are ready to understand."

Almanza glanced over her shoulder at Moyo and Nia. They both stood silently, their unwavering support evident in their expressions. Moyo gave her a nod, a silent reassurance, while Nia's smile was small but filled with quiet strength. Almanza felt a surge of gratitude for their presence—she was not alone in this moment.

With a deep breath, Almanza turned back to the fire, its flames now rising higher, twisting in patterns that seemed to mirror the uncertainty in her heart. She closed her eyes for a moment, centering herself, and then stepped into the circle of light.

As her feet touched the ground near the fire, the air grew heavier, the heat from the flames now suffusing her skin, her soul. The whispers that had surrounded the village seemed to grow louder, faint voices drifting on the wind, murmuring words she could not quite understand. She opened her eyes and looked into the flames.

They shifted and swirled, transforming into images—visions of her past, her mother's face, the storm, the ancient spirits that had bound their fates together. The faces of the villagers, the burning fire, the flashes of green eyes, all blending into one blurred image that made her head spin. The flames were no longer just fire; they were alive, telling a story older than the land itself.

Almanza's hand reached out instinctively, as if drawn by an invisible force, and the flames parted before her, revealing a figure standing in the heart of the fire—her mother.

A sharp gasp escaped her lips as she stepped forward, her breath caught in her throat. The woman before her was beautiful, with long dark hair flowing like a river of night and eyes that sparkled with the same intense green that Almanza herself carried. But it was her presence that struck Almanza most—the ethereal quality, as if she were not entirely of this world, but something more, something powerful.

"Mother," Almanza whispered, her voice trembling.

The woman's lips curved into a soft smile, a gesture that held both sadness and understanding. "You have come, my child," she said, her voice a soft melody that seemed to reverberate through the very core of Almanza's being. "I knew you would. I felt it the moment you were born, that you would seek me, seek the truth."

Almanza's heart ached with longing, a feeling of loss so deep it threatened to swallow her whole. "Why? Why did you leave me? Why did you hide from me?"

The woman's gaze softened with a sorrow that mirrored Almanza's own. "I never wanted to leave you, child. But the world is filled with dangers that few understand, and I had to protect you. I had to give you the strength to survive on your own."

"But I'm not strong enough. I've been searching for answers my whole life, and I don't know who I am, what I'm meant to do..." Almanza's voice faltered, her chest tight with emotion. "I don't understand."

The woman stepped closer, her presence warm and calming, yet distant, as if there were an invisible wall between them. "You are my legacy, Almanza. The strength you seek lies within you already. You were born with the blood of the ancients, of those who once controlled the elements, who shaped the world with their will. You carry their power, and with it, the responsibility to protect what is sacred."

Almanza's mind raced, the weight of her mother's words settling over her like a storm. "But I don't know how to control it. I don't know how to protect anything."

Her mother's eyes shone with a knowing light. "That is why you've come to Shongwe, why you've journeyed this far. The truth is not always easy, my child, but it is the key to unlocking your power. The fire, the land, the spirits—they are all connected to you. The path you walk will be difficult, but you will find your way."

Tears welled up in Almanza's eyes as she stepped forward, her heart breaking at the thought of all the lost years, of a mother she never truly knew. "I don't know if I'm ready for all of this. I don't know if I can do what you ask."

Her mother's expression softened with an undeniable tenderness. "You are ready, Almanza. You always have been. The power within you has been waiting for this moment, for you to claim it. But you must be willing to accept all of who you are, the darkness and the light, the truth and the pain."

With those final words, the fire began to fade, the flames retracting back into the earth, leaving only a lingering warmth in their place. The vision of her mother slowly dissolved, like smoke on the wind, until she was nothing but a memory—one Almanza would carry with her always.

Almanza stood in the fading light, her heart heavy but full. She felt a new sense of clarity, a deep knowing that she had not come all this way for nothing. The truth had been revealed to her, and while it was not easy, it was necessary.

Moyo and Nia approached her, their faces filled with concern, but also understanding. Moyo placed a hand on her shoulder, his voice low and reassuring. "Are you alright?"

Almanza nodded slowly, her gaze far away, but her voice steady. "I understand now. I know what I have to do."

Nia stepped closer, her voice soft but resolute. "We're with you, no matter what. You don't have to carry this burden alone."

Almanza turned to face them, her eyes shining with determination. "Thank you. Together, we'll face whatever comes next."

As the sun dipped below the horizon, casting the village in a soft, golden glow, Almanza felt a shift within herself—a deep and profound change. She had stepped into the shadows of her past and emerged with the strength to walk into the future. And with her friends by her side, she was ready to face whatever came next.

The flames of truth had burned away the doubts and fears, leaving only the promise of what was to come. The path ahead was uncertain, but Almanza knew one thing for sure: she was no longer alone.

And the shadows that had once haunted her now stood as stepping stones to her destiny.

Chapter Nineteen

The Grove of Memories

As dawn's light filtered softly through the trees, Almanza made her way to the secluded grove at the edge of Maputo. This place, known as the Grove of Memories, was steeped in history a space where the village elders came to seek counsel from their ancestors and where the spirits of Maputo's lineage were said to linger.

Almanza felt a mixture of anticipation and reverence as she approached the grove. Towering ancient trees stood like silent sentries, their gnarled branches forming a canopy overhead that allowed only small patches of sunlight to seep through. She could feel the hum of the land, as if the very earth was alive with whispers from ages past.

"Is this really the place, Nia?" she asked her companion, her voice barely more than a whisper. Her friend Nia, who had grown up listening to tales of the grove's power, gave a nod.

"It's said that the spirits of those who came before us linger here, that they sometimes appear to those who seek wisdom," Nia replied, her gaze steady. "Perhaps they'll hear you too, Almanza."

Taking a deep breath, Almanza walked deeper into the grove. She could feel the energy shift around her, a subtle but unmistakable weight in the air that spoke of unseen presences. The trees themselves seemed to lean closer, as if to witness her journey. Almanza knelt at the base of an ancient baobab, closing her eyes and grounding herself to the earth.

"Please," she whispered, her voice trembling with a mixture of awe and yearning. "I seek guidance... I seek... you."

As she stilled her mind, a warmth crept through her, and the grove around her softened, the light shifting into a gentle glow. In her mind's eye, she saw hazy forms emerging from the mist—warriors, healers, rulers, each bearing marks of power and wisdom. The air grew thick with their presence, filling her with a deep sense of connection and comfort.

A figure stepped forward, and Almanza's heart leapt. She recognized her mother, Nandi, from the stories and visions she had seen in dreams. Nandi's face held the strength of a warrior and the tenderness of a mother's love, her eyes full of a warmth that Almanza hadn't realized she'd longed for until this moment.

"Almanza," Nandi's voice echoed softly, carrying both strength and compassion. "I've watched you from beyond, proud and vigilant. You carry within you a power beyond what you see. And yet, this power is not yours alone—it is the legacy of all those who came before you."

Almanza struggled to hold back tears. "Mother... I don't know if I'm ready for this. Sometimes, it feels like the power is too vast, like it wants to consume me."

Nandi knelt beside her, brushing a gentle hand over her cheek. "Power can indeed be overwhelming. It is a river, Almanza, sometimes swift and unforgiving. But it is not here to drown you—it is here to guide you, if you learn to listen to its current."

Almanza looked down, her fingers tracing patterns in the soil. "I'm afraid... afraid of becoming something I don't recognize, something that might hurt the ones I love. I feel this growing distance between me and the villagers, even though I want to protect them."

Nandi's expression softened, her gaze filled with both pride and sorrow. "That fear, my daughter, is not a weakness; it is your strength. Those who wield power without fear often lack the wisdom to wield it well. And you, Almanza, possess the wisdom of restraint, the awareness of humility."

A soft rustling signaled the approach of another figure. Nia and Moyo, two of her closest friends, had found her in the grove. They stood quietly, sensing the reverence in the air, their eyes wide as they saw the faint outline of Nandi beside Almanza.

Nia took a cautious step forward. "Almanza... is that...?"

Almanza nodded, her voice choked with emotion. "It is my mother. She... she's here."

Moyo stepped closer, bowing his head in respect to the spirit of Nandi. "We came looking for you. We thought you might need someone to lean on."

Nandi's gaze shifted to Nia and Moyo, her expression one of approval. "These friends are your strength, Almanza. You are not meant to carry this alone."

Almanza looked at her friends, feeling the depth of her gratitude for their loyalty. "Thank you, both of you. Sometimes, I feel like the power sets me apart from everyone. But with you, I feel... grounded."

Nandi's voice was soft but firm. "The weight of power will always be heavy, Almanza. But remember that you are not defined by it. You are defined by your choices, your heart, and those who stand by you. Your legacy is not only in your magic but in the love you nurture and protect."

Almanza looked up, a flicker of hope rising within her. "Then I will carry this weight with humility, Mother. I will learn to master it, not as a queen, but as a protector of Maputo."

Nandi gave her a proud smile, her form beginning to waver as the light around her softened. "You have the courage of many, my child. Walk with that strength, and know that we are always here, guiding you."

Almanza reached out, her voice thick with emotion. "Will I see you again?"

Nandi's figure faded, her voice lingering like a whisper in the breeze. "I am always with you, my daughter, as are all who came before. Trust in yourself, and you will never walk alone."

As the vision dissolved, Almanza found herself surrounded by the comforting silence of the grove once more. Her friends remained by her side, their expressions a mix of awe and respect.

"Almanza," Nia said, breaking the silence gently. "Whatever you need, we're here for you. You don't have to shoulder this alone."

Moyo nodded, his gaze steady. "We trust you, and we believe in you. Just remember that the village stands with you, even if they don't fully understand your power."

Almanza felt a deep peace settle within her. She no longer felt alone, no longer burdened by a power that seemed beyond her control. She had her mother's guidance, her ancestors' legacy, and the unwavering support of her friends.

"Thank you," she murmured, her heart filled with a new resolve. "With all of you by my side, I feel ready to face whatever comes."

They left the grove together, the rising sun casting a warm glow over Maputo. And as they walked back toward the village, Almanza felt the weight of her power balanced by the strength of her bonds, a harmony that she knew would guide her in the trials to come.

As Almanza, Nia, and Moyo made their way back from the Grove of Memories, they moved in a comfortable silence, each absorbed in their thoughts. The encounter with Nandi had given Almanza a renewed sense of purpose, but it also stirred emotions she hadn't fully faced—the lingering ache of abandonment, the sudden clarity of her destiny, and the vast responsibility that lay ahead.

The village was beginning to stir with early morning activity as they entered Maputo. Farmers readied their tools, children played near the wells, and the market bustled with preparations. The villagers noticed Almanza's return, their eyes flickering with a mixture of respect and curiosity.

Nia glanced at Almanza, sensing her unease. "They admire you, you know," she whispered. "Even if some are wary, they know you're here for them."

Almanza nodded, trying to shake off the tension. "I just hope they see my intentions clearly. The last thing I want is for them to be afraid of me."

Moyo, always the calm voice of reason, offered a reassuring smile. "Fear fades with understanding, Almanza. The more they see you as one of their own, the more they'll accept your gifts. Trust takes time."

As they walked, Queen Adisa emerged from the palace, her regal presence a comforting sight amid Almanza's inner turmoil. She beckoned them over, her eyes studying her daughter intently.

"Almanza," Adisa began, her tone both gentle and firm, "did you find what you were seeking?"

Almanza met her mother's gaze, feeling the weight of everything she'd experienced. "Yes, Mama. I... I spoke to the spirits. I saw her. Nandi was there."

Adisa's eyes softened, her expression unreadable. "Your birth mother. I can only imagine how that must have felt."

Almanza took a deep breath, grounding herself. "It gave me peace, Mama. She reminded me that this power isn't just mine—that it's part of our people, our ancestors. I am only a vessel for something much larger."

Adisa nodded approvingly, placing a gentle hand on Almanza's shoulder. "That wisdom will serve you well, my child. Remember, this power can either bind you to the people or set you apart. It's your choice how you use it."

Nia and Moyo, sensing the importance of this moment, stepped back to give mother and daughter space.

Almanza looked up at her mother, a question that had been weighing on her mind finally surfacing. "Mama, do you ever fear... that this power might take me down a path you didn't intend?"

Adisa's expression grew serious, her eyes filled with both love and resolve. "Fear is natural, Almanza. I worried the day I took you in, knowing you came from another lineage, that perhaps one day you might seek that history. But I trusted that love and guidance would ground you. And so far, you've shown me nothing but courage and strength."

"It's just..." Almanza hesitated, glancing down at her hands, which still tingled faintly from the energy she'd wielded in the grove. "Sometimes I feel like the power is too vast, too consuming. Like it could slip from my control at any moment."

Adisa's voice softened, her gaze full of empathy. "Power can be overwhelming, and there will always be moments of doubt. But Almanza, remember what your mother said: you are part of a legacy. You are not alone in this, and you never will be."

Almanza nodded, feeling a new wave of determination rise within her. "Thank you, Mama. I'll remember that."

Just then, one of the village elders approached them. Elder Bayo, who had long been a trusted advisor to Adisa, bowed respectfully before addressing them.

"Your Majesty, Almanza," he began, his tone grave, "the council has been discussing the recent events—the storm, the damage, and what it means for our village. They... they have questions about the nature of Almanza's powers."

Almanza tensed, feeling the familiar prickle of uncertainty. Adisa, sensing her daughter's discomfort, placed a reassuring hand on her shoulder.

"Thank you, Elder Bayo," Adisa said smoothly. "Almanza and I will speak with the council. They deserve to understand what we face."

The elder nodded, his expression softening. "Of course, Your Majesty. Almanza, know that you have allies in the council. We believe in you."

Almanza offered him a grateful smile, feeling the weight of her role settling on her shoulders once more. She looked to her mother, her heart steady with a new resolve.

"I'm ready to speak with them, Mama," she said firmly. "They deserve to hear the truth from me."

Adisa smiled, pride shining in her eyes. "Then let's go, my daughter. Together, we'll face whatever comes."

With her friends close behind, Almanza followed her mother to the council chamber. As they walked through the village square, she felt a surge of strength and purpose. The vision of her mother and the voices of her ancestors echoed within her, grounding her. She was no longer just a girl with powers—she was a protector of Maputo, bound by love, legacy, and a promise that would shape the future of her village.

And as they entered the council chamber, Almanza knew that, no matter the challenges ahead, she was ready to embrace the path destiny had set before her.

CHAPTER TWENTY

Bloodline Unveiled

ALMANZA, FLANKED BY HER dearest friends Nia, Kofi and Moyo, walked with a sense of calm purpose as she reached the heart of Shongwe. The village was alive with an ancient energy, one that seemed to hum in the air and whisper through the trees. Her heart beat with anticipation—this was the moment she had been waiting for, the moment to unravel the mysteries of her past. Nia leaned close, sensing Almanza's nervous excitement. "You've been waiting for this your whole life, Almanza. I can see it in your eyes. Are you... ready?" Almanza took a deep breath, her gaze steady as she looked at her friends. "More ready than ever. Whatever I find out today,

I know it's only going to make me stronger. And it means everything to have you both here with me." Kofi grinned, his usual lighthearted demeanor giving way to a sense of gravity. "We wouldn't miss this for the world. Besides, who else will help you make sense of all this ancient mystery?" They approached the elder's hut, a structure adorned with symbols and carvings that seemed to hold secrets of ages past. The elder, a dignified man with a wise, knowing gaze, welcomed them with a slight nod, his eyes lingering on Almanza with a familiarity she could not yet understand. "Almanza," he greeted, his voice both warm and filled with reverence. "You've come seeking answers, and it's time you know the truth of your lineage." Almanza felt a thrill of anticipation mixed with trepidation. "Please... tell me everything." The elder motioned for them to sit around a low, crackling fire. He began his story, his voice weaving a tale that stretched across generations. "Almanza, your birth was no ordinary event. You are the product of a love that defied boundaries—a love between your mother, Nandi, and a royal bloodline she was never meant to touch." Almanza's eyes widened, her heart thudding in her chest. "Royal bloodline...?" The elder nodded, a faint smile playing on his lips. "Yes. Your father was not just anyone—he was the brother of Queen Adisa."

Her mind reeled at the revelation. "So... Queen Adisa is my aunt?" Nia and Kofi exchanged stunned glances, and Kofi was the first to break the silence. "Whoa... so you really are royalty, Almanza!" Almanza took a deep breath, trying to absorb the weight of this truth. Her voice was soft, filled with awe. "All this time, and I never knew." The elder continued, his voice dropping to a near whisper. "Your parents' love was forbidden, and because of that, a curse was cast upon your lineage—a curse that would affect not only you but the powers you carry. Your blood holds both light and shadow, and that is why your magic feels as though it carries two sides." Almanza looked down at her hands, memories of her powers' fierce duality flashing through her mind. "So... the light and the darkness in me... it's part of my bloodline?" The elder nodded. "Yes. Your destiny is bound to both. But you are not defined by either alone. You have the power to choose your own path, to use both light and shadow to protect and to heal." Almanza felt a new strength rise within her—a sense of purpose that she had never fully grasped until now. "Thank you... thank you for telling me this." She looked up at Nia and Kofi, her eyes shining. "It means I can embrace who I am, every part of it." Nia reached over, squeezing her hand. "Almanza, you were always destined for greatness. Knowing your past only makes your light shine brighter." Kofi added with a grin, "And now you have even more reason to keep us around—we're practically family!" The elder watched them with a soft smile before speaking again. "Almanza, there's one more thing. Your mothers—both Nandi and Queen Adisa—deserve to meet each other. To know that their shared love has given you the strength to fulfill your destiny." Almanza felt her heart leap. "Yes... I want them both to know. They're both my family." The elder gave a nod of approval. "Then let it be so. Your journey is no longer just about discovering your past. It's about uniting the parts of yourself, embracing your legacy, and fulfilling the role you were born to play." The next morning, with Nandi by her side, Almanza made her way back to Maputo, her heart racing with joy and anticipation. As they entered the palace grounds, Queen Adisa emerged, her gaze softening as she saw them approach. "Your Majesty," Almanza began, her voice filled with gratitude and excitement, "I have someone you need to meet." Queen Adisa's gaze shifted to Nandi, and in that moment, something unspoken passed between them—a shared understanding, a recognition of the love that had brought Almanza into the world. "Nandi," Adisa greeted, her voice warm and steady, "thank you for raising her, for bringing her to this point." Nandi's eyes shone with pride and humility. "And thank you, Queen Adisa, for loving her as your own. She is all the more powerful because she has two mothers who cherish her." Almanza looked between the two women, her heart swelling with happiness. "I'm so grateful to have both of you in my life. I promise, I'll make you proud. I'll embrace everything you've taught me—both of you—and I'll carry our legacy forward." As she spoke, a fierce determination lit her gaze, her voice filled with strength and confidence. "I now understand my journey isn't just about me. I am the link between two worlds, the legacy of two families. And I will honor both sides of my heritage." Queen Adisa placed a hand on her shoulder, her expression filled with pride. "Almanza, you are a protector, a healer, and a bridge between past and future. Your strength comes from all of us, and we are with you always." Nandi stepped forward, her voice filled with emotion. "You have my love, my blessing, and my faith, my daughter. Let the world see the light and shadow within you, and may you always remember who you are." Almanza felt a sense of peace settle over her. With Nia, Kofi, Moyo and her mothers by her side, she knew she was ready for whatever lay ahead. She looked out over the village, her heart brimming with gratitude and purpose."This is only the beginning," she whispered to herself, feeling the thrill of the journey that awaited her. "The story isn't over." As the sun rose higher in the sky, Almanza knew that this was a moment she would carry forever. Her heart was full, her spirit strong, and her legacy secured. And as the winds whispered through the trees, she could almost hear the voices of her ancestors urging her forward, guiding her into a future filled with both light and shadow, love and strength.As Almanza stood between her two mothers, she felt a warmth radiating from within—a power that transcended magic, a strength born from love, and a determination rooted in legacy. She looked out at the village of Maputo, the place that had become her home and the people she was bound to protect. The journey she had been on—the questions, the struggles, the discoveries—had all led her to this moment, and she felt a new fire kindling inside her.Queen Adisa broke the silence, her voice steady and filled with emotion. "Almanza, you have been blessed with not only powerful gifts but also the wisdom to use them wisely. I have no doubt that you will face whatever comes with courage and integrity. But remember," she added, her gaze turning serious, "power will continue to test you, and so will those who seek to use it for their own ends." Almanza nodded, her eyes meeting Adisa's with a fierce resolve. "I understand, Mama. I know now that my power isn't just for me—it's for Maputo, for the legacy I carry, and for the world beyond. I'll honor it, and I'll protect it." Nandi, watching her daughter with pride, stepped forward, her voice barely a whisper yet full of intensity. "And we will be by your side, no matter what. Both of us, your family, your friends—we are all here, Almanza." "Thank you," Almanza replied, her voice thick with emotion. "For everything." Just then, Nia and Kofi, who had been watching quietly, joined them, bringing with them a youthful energy that lifted the weight of the moment. "So," Nia said, her eyes twinkling, "does this mean we're officially part of the royal family now, too?" Kofi chuckled, his grin infectious. "Seems like it! And it means we have to stick together, even more than before." He looked at Almanza, his face turning serious for a moment. "You've got us, always. Whatever challenges come, we're in it together." Almanza laughed, the tension of the day easing as she looked at her friends, who had been by her side through every twist and turn. "I couldn't ask for anything more. With both of you, with my mothers, and with everyone here... I feel like I can face anything." As the sun began to set, casting golden hues over Maputo, the group turned toward the village square. Villagers gathered, their expressions filled with both curiosity and anticipation, sensing that something monumental had transpired. Queen Adisa stepped forward, raising her voice so that all could hear. "People of Maputo, today we celebrate a revelation and the beginning of a new chapter. Almanza, my daughter, is not only a member of our royal family but also a descendant of a powerful lineage, a protector whose gifts are meant to serve our people. " The crowd murmured, absorbing this revelation. They looked at Almanza with a newfound respect, their awe mixed with pride. One by one, they bowed their heads, acknowledging her role in their lives. Almanza felt a sense of calm wash over her, knowing that her people accepted her fully, both as one of their own and as something extraordinary. Just then, Elder Bayo stepped forward, his face breaking into a smile as he addressed Almanza. "The spirits of our ancestors are rejoicing tonight, Almanza.

You are the embodiment of their hopes and their struggles. You have brought honor to both your families, and to us all. Nandi took Almanza's hand, her voice soft but carrying a strength that resonated with everyone present.

"And let this be known—no matter what trials come, no matter what dangers lie ahead, my daughter will stand tall. She is a bridge between worlds, a child of light and shadow. She is meant to lead." Almanza, feeling the weight of the words, closed her eyes briefly, gathering her thoughts. When she spoke, her voice was steady and clear, carrying across the square. "Thank you, everyone. I am honored by your trust and your love. I promise, as long as I draw breath, I will protect Maputo. I will protect all of you." The villagers erupted in cheers, a wave of unity and joy sweeping over them. For the first time, Almanza felt truly at peace with her role, her power, and her future.As the celebration continued, Nia, Kofi, Moyo and Almanza huddled together, a glint of mischief in their eyes. "So, Almanza," Nia began, her voice teasing, "now that you're a queen and all, what's our first adventure?" Almanza laughed, her eyes sparkling. "Adventure? How about a night of celebration? We've all earned it." Kofi grinned, nudging her playfully. "Just one request, though. When it's time for the next big quest, make sure we're right there beside you." Almanza's smile softened, filled with gratitude and joy. "Always. You're my family, too." And as they laughed and planned, Almanza felt a thrill of excitement for the future. Her journey was far from over—in many ways, it was just beginning. The night was filled with laughter, warmth, and the promise of the adventures yet to come. And with her family, her friends, and her village by her side, Almanza knew that she was ready for whatever lay ahead.The stars twinkled above, a thousand silent witnesses to her vow, and somewhere in the depths of the night, the spirits of her ancestors looked on with pride, knowing that their legacy was in the hands of one who would honor it with courage, love, and boundless strength.

Epilogue

The morning air was crisp as Almanza stood on the outskirts of Maputo, her eyes fixed on the horizon where the first light of dawn painted the sky in shades of pink and gold. The village was quiet, still wrapped in the calm of early morning, and the familiar sounds of birdsong filled the air. Red Bird, her constant companion, perched nearby, its gaze as watchful as ever.

Almanza turned, taking in the sight of her friends and family—Nia and Kofi, who had been with her through every twist and turn; Queen Adisa, her steadfast mother; and Nandi, her birth mother, who had returned to guide her and stand by her side.

"Are you ready?" Queen Adisa asked, her voice gentle but resolute.

Almanza nodded, a smile tugging at the corner of her mouth. "Yes. It's time for me to see what lies beyond Maputo's borders." She had learned so much, but she knew her journey had only just begun. There was a world beyond the village, a world that needed protectors, healers, and the balance she could bring.

Nandi stepped forward, placing a comforting hand on her shoulder. "Remember, you carry the strength of two mothers and the love of those who came before you. Whatever you face, you are never truly alone."

As the sun climbed higher, the villagers gathered to bid farewell to their protector, their expressions filled with pride and hope. Almanza turned to Nia and Kofi, who grinned at her, their eyes alight with anticipation.

"You're not leaving without us, right?" Kofi teased, nudging her shoulder.

Almanza laughed, the sound warm and free. "Of course not. This adventure wouldn't be the same without you two."

With one last look at Maputo, Almanza took a step forward, her heart brimming with joy and excitement for the unknown. She was no longer just the girl with green eyes. She was a protector, a healer, and a descendant of those who had paved the way. And as she walked, the spirits of her ancestors whispered through the breeze, guiding her onward, her destiny awaiting just beyond the horizon.

Connect with the Author

 Please Please Please , Don't forget to leave a review.. Thank you so so much for your support

. https://rebrand.ly/Destiny-Review

Dive deeper into the world of storytelling, inspiration, and empowerment with Ms. LJ Hall, PhD. Stay connected to explore new works, behind-the-scenes insights, and engaging content that brings stories to life.

Website: msljhall.com
YouTube: In The Know with Ms. LJ Hall, PhD
Media & Booking Inquiries: booking@msljhall.com

Support the Journey: buymeacoffee.com/MsLJHall

Don't miss out! Subscribe, follow, and support for updates on upcoming books, exclusive videos, and more! Let's continue this journey together.

Meet The Author

Ms. LJ Hall, PhD is an author, educator, and entrepreneur with a passion for storytelling and empowering others. A Detroit native, she discovered her love for writing at a young age, crafting stories that helped her navigate a challenging childhood. Today, she draws from her diverse experiences to create tales of resilience, courage, and self-discovery. In addition to writing, she enjoys traveling, performing improv, and spending time with her beloved dog, Bella. Eyes of Destiny: Journey of Almanza is her latest work, inviting readers into a journey of magic, heritage, and destiny.

Acknowledgements

FIRST AND FOREMOST, I want to thank God for guiding my path and being my light through every step of this journey. I've been through so much, and yet, You've always shown me that every challenge and triumph is a part of Your divine plan. Your grace and presence have carried me through, and I am forever grateful.

Completing this book has been a journey of transformation, healing, and growth, and I could not have done it without the incredible people who supported me along the way. Each of you played a significant role in lifting me up, and I am forever grateful.

Anastasia – You have always been there when I needed you the most. You are an amazing mother and friend, and I am so grateful that God brought us closer together. Your love and support saved my life—Literally!!!! Thank you for being my rock and for helping me breathe when it felt impossible.

Dionisia – I can't believe it's been over 25 years (even though we're still only 25, of course!). Your friendship has been such a blessing in my life. You've been my confidant, my cheerleader, and my voice of reason. I hope one day I can be as great a friend to you as you've been to me. Your kindness and strength inspire me daily.

Tatiana – You are my wild child, and I love you for it! Thank you for letting me be myself around you and for always bringing laughter and energy to my life. You're truly one of a kind, and I'm so lucky to have you in my corner.

Monique and Lisa – You both met me at a time when I was broken and bruised, and instead of walking away, you lifted me up. Your friendship brought me strength and light when I needed it most. Thank you for always being down to ride and for making me feel whole again.

LeAnn – You are an incredible sister and friend. Thank you for your kindness, love, and unwavering support. Your presence gave me the peace I needed to keep going, and I'll always be thankful for you.

Auntie Armelia – Thank you for your love and support, which mean so much to me. I know I need to get better at calling, but please know I carry your love with me always.

Mother Blair – I am so proud to call you my other mother. Your open heart and generosity have been a source of strength and inspiration to me. Thank you for being such a wonderful example of kindness and love.

Bella – To my loyal companion and writing buddy, Ruff Ruff, Thank you for being by my side through every late night and every word written. Your presence brought me comfort and peace in ways only you could. Ruff Ruff

Kristosser and Kiesha – My cousin and my dear friend, your lives were taken far too soon. I will always cherish the time we had together and carry your memories in my heart. I hope this book makes your souls smile. I miss you both so much.

Adrienne – Though our paths have since diverged, I want to sincerely thank you for being there during one of the hardest times in my life. Your support in that season meant more to me than I can ever express. I will always hold gratitude for the help and kindness you showed me when I needed it most. Wishing you peace and blessings on your journey.

My YouTube Subscribers – Thank you for being part of my journey. Your support, encouragement, and connection have been a big part of my growth, and I appreciate each and every one of you.

This book is a reflection of the love, kindness, and strength you've all shared with me. Thank you for helping me turn my dreams into reality.

Made in the USA
Columbia, SC
11 February 2025

53453640R00195